MW01706870

Perimeters

A Novel of Mystery

Patricia Gehman

PublishAmerica
Baltimore

First printing.

ISBN: 1-4137-4432-X
PUBLISHED BY PUBLISHAMERICA, LLLP
www.publishamerica.com
Baltimore

Printed in the United States of America

To my late beloved parents,
Frank and Helen Siehler
You are always in my heart.

Acknowledgments
A special thanks to all of my friends and relatives who encouraged me to never stop writing. To my daughter Lauren, I give my love for her continuing support and encouragement.

1

If you were to have gone to the end of the world, taken a left and gone four miles, you would have arrived there. Mercyville, where a light mist crept across the valley, and dotted among the hemlock-covered mountains were a few scattered lights from the cabins to the north. To the east, lights were coming from the barn of Sam Sell's dairy farm. With over fifty heads of cows, the workday often continued well into the night.

Looking west, the outline of West Knob mansion was being devoured by the enveloping fog. The lights on the pillars at the front gates still shone through the gray mist. The house was almost dark with the exception of the light coming from the massive entrance hall. In the distance, a coyote howled in search of its mate. Close to her house, she could hear the whimpers of the pure white buck deer calling to the doe and feel the stillness of the night settling over the valley. From the little white church at the end of the road came the sounds of long forgotten hymns spreading softly through the air. The same scene was repeated time and again, night after night, as Mercyville settled into the Prussian blue cloak of the final part of day.

The forty-five year-old, free spirited, Alison Wallace loved it here with its peace and quiet. There were no more crowds, no more hour-long lines of traffic, no more high-priced coffee shops and over-priced housing. And finally, there was no more rushing to a boring, dead-end job. This was the Garden of Eden for Alison and her husband, Matt. Now they were both finally free to explore the resources of their minds and free to bring them to life. They both loved art and now they had the freedom and time to pursue their dreams.

When the night sky lifted, trails of dust could be seen on the secondary roads across the valley as some of the residents of Mercyville headed out of the mountains to their jobs in the city. Jobs were few and far between so most of the young people left the mountains in search of better opportunities in the cities. There were a few lumber mills scattered through out the Endless Mountains and those that didn't work at the mills, usually ended working for the Highway department. Dotted up and down the valleys were five or six Bed and Breakfast homes trying to eke out a living from the summer and fall tourists. During hunting season they were usually full, as were most of the second-home cabins of the city people.

The village consisted of a combination post-office/country store. Branching out, it now had a newly added patio with umbrella tables, where the summer tourists and locals could enjoy ice cream and sandwiches. Across the road stood an out-of-business flower shop. Looking up hill from the post-office, one could see the spiral of the Mercyville church. About a mile to the east, there was a recreation ground which was practically empty in mid-winter, but swelled to over three hundred during the rest of the year.

The recreation ground had a small grocery store and had recently started providing sandwiches, soups and pizza; the best pizza anywhere in the Endless Mountains. On the far north end of the village stood a refurbished cream colored Victorian house set off with cranberry gingerbread trim. There was a rejuvenated old barn setting to the rear of the property, which served as an antique shop. A half-mile east of the church was the Volunteer Fire Department, which was also utilized as a gathering place for the Endless Mountains breakfasts, dinners and numerous other social events. As a visitor, driving through Mercyville, you would wonder how many people lived there. But on special occasions, going to church, trips to town or just visiting neighbors, those hidden deep within the swells of hemlock and dogwoods, would emerge. There was definitely no lack of modern transportation, as the latest motor vehicles drove out from beneath the lacey canopies of green. Many of the families of Mercyville had been there for generations; some dating back to the eighteen hundreds. This was substantiated on the headstones of the small, well-kept local cemetery. People of the area were thrifty and worked hard all of their lives. If someone was in need, the village turned to help.

Comradery could be seen at the coffee shop, which was connected, to the post-office/country store. Actually, it couldn't be classified as a shop, but consisted of an over-sized round table near an always on coffeepot. It was here news of the community was circulated and the men made major decisions, at least that was what the women of the village thought.

Every morning the men made their way in to the store and speculated on just about anything that came to mind. If there were ten men, there were that many opinions on any given subject. Alison's husband, Matt, was among the conclave of opinion makers. He had been an illustrator for a major advertising agency and was equally as glad as she was to settle in to a less stress-filled life.

Their house, with seven acres of land, sat on top of a high plateau in the Endless Mountains. The view was breathtaking, especially in the fall when the leaves turned the mountains into layers of crimson, gold and orange. Their guests envied the beauty and serenity of the small homestead.

The cycle of life in Mercyville was that of any place else. Birth, struggling through life with both joys and sorrows, and finally death. Nothing of national importance could be attributed to Mercyville and the natives were happy to keep it that way. Any change to the village would come in a slow, progressive-conservative approach with a consensus of local opinion.

Mercyville was the Plain-Jane of towns and villages. At least that was how it was conceived to be until a month ago.

No longer were the doors left unlocked and now the children were guarded even more closely. The locals were cautious of non-residents, whether or not it was warranted. They were looked upon with suspicion and only slowly were they drawn into any form of trust. It had not always been that way, but recent circumstances forced the locals in to that position.

Without a trace, two young women of the Mercyville area had disappeared. Weeks of searching and questioning had turned up absolutely nothing. It seemed as though the though they had vanished into thin air.

Mary McCarty was nineteen and home from college on spring vacation. She was a tall, beautiful, blonde, young woman with blue eyes that sparkled when she spoke. It was seven o'clock in the evening when she left her parent's home to visit a friend in Edwardton just eleven miles away. She never arrived. Her car was found just west of Mercyville. There was not a single clue as to what could have happened to her. Her purse was in the car and the keys were still in the ignition.

Two days later, twenty-year-old Leslie Vermillion met the same fate. She and her husband had been married for less than a year. She worked at the Edwardton bank and left work, as usual, at five o'clock for the eleven mile drive home. Like Mary McCarty, her car was found by the side of the road with her purse and keys inside. She was only six miles from her home. Not only were the police looking for Mary, but now they were also searching for Leslie. For almost two weeks hundreds of people joined in the monumental search but it turned up nothing. The police had exhausted every available avenue of resource in the investigation, but now the case was turning cold. Her husband, Sam, even hired a private detective from Philadelphia but he, like the police, came up empty handed.

Since the disappearance of the two women, the comradery of the coffee shop had become a lot more somber. No one had a clue as to what could have happened to the women. Every second-home cabin in a ten mile radius had been searched, but to no avail. At this point, none of the residents of Mercyville were suspects and none of them knew of any part-time residents who could have been involved in the disappearances. This type of crime was definitely out of character for the peaceful community.

Mercyville was on guard for the first time in over one hundred and fifty years.

2

Outside of the beauty of the Endless Mountains themselves there was only one above average tourist spot, to view, in the Village of Mercyville. Four miles west of the centrally located post office, was West Knob mansion. It was surrounded by a sprawling two hundred and fifty acres of lush, towering hemlocks, dogwood, birch, oak and dozens of flowering shrubs and bushes. It was the home of dozens of species of birds and wild animals. The house itself sat on an open plateau on the very top of the mountain. The mansion was built in 1880 by Charles Devon's great-grandfather, Albert Devon, the founder of the Philadelphia Devon Furniture Empire. The mansion stood like a sentinel watching over the village.

At the entrance to West Knob there was a heavy, intricately carved wooden gate that was flanked on both sides with two high stone columns. On top of each column stood a mammoth carriage type lamp, which had been imported, from Italy. As you went through the gate and up the half-mile long driveway, it was lined on both sides with ancient oak trees. The huge two-story stone house had a sprawling front porch and four white columns supporting a large second floor balcony. As you entered there was a massive central entrance hall with a wide staircase. To the right was a gigantic living room with windows looking out over the valley of Mercyville. On the second floor there were five large bedrooms, each having its own view of the surrounding mountains. It was here at West Knob that the generations of Devon's had spent some of the happiest years of their lives. In the mountains, the children were free to explore the beautiful natural environment.

In 1975, upon the death of his Father, the handsome young thirty-three-year-old, Charles Devon, became the sole owner of the Devon furniture dynasty. They had built their fortune on the beautifully designed and intricately carved furniture. The Devon's only hired the finest craftsmen who they handsomely rewarded. Charles, like those before him, had the same innate sense of design and an astute mind for business. He expanded the family business by opening six stores dedicated to the promotion of the Devon fine furniture. Two of the stores were in Philadelphia, one in New York and three were in Baltimore. Within a year, the demands for the magnificent furniture had doubled.

In1976, Charles married Rebecca Mattison. In contrast to her tall, stately husband with his dark hair and eyes, Rebecca was blonde with green eyes and had a youthful exuberance. Three years later, the union had produced two sons, Joseph and Paul.

Through the years both Charles and Rebecca indulged their sons, providing their every need. They attended the most prestigious schools and colleges. At an early age, Joseph knew he would follow in his father's footsteps. He was highly creative and yet had an earnest mind for business, while Paul was like his mother and was endowed with a love of the outdoors and animals. He had an acute ability to communicate with the wild fauna and even the whitetail deer at West Knob allowed him to approach them. He, like his brother, also knew at an early age what path he would pursue. His choice would be that of veterinary medicine. With a passion for horses, he spent almost every minute at West Knob in the saddle exploring the mountains surrounding Mercyville.

Even though the brothers were almost opposites, they were practically inseparable. Paul idolized his older brother, Joseph, and both would have given his life for the other.

It seemed to the people of Mercyville that the Devon family, the Aristocrats of the Mountains, had everything: money, prestige and most of all a loving family. But during the months prior to the disappearance of McCarty and Vermillion, the Devon family had suffered their own misfortunes.

It was early August, 1998 and as they had done for the past twenty-five years, the family had opened up the mansion at West Knob for the summer. Joseph, now twenty-two and Paul now twenty-one, were anxious to leave Philadelphia and the pressures of college. They always looked forward to leaving the confines of city for the summer and going to West Knob where they could breathe the cool mountain air and spend time in the outdoors. Early on an August morning, the two brothers went to the converted carriage house and saddled up two of the horses for a leisurely ride through the mountains. Riding through the hemlock forest they had a sense of freedom that they could not find anywhere else. It was here that they enjoyed the same pleasures of the outdoors as their ancestors.

As they rode through the woods, they spotted several new fawns and as the horses approached, they darted into the thick forest. Paul had a special rapport with a white buck deer that lived at West Knob. The young buck would let Paul get within touching distance to him and they seemed to be kindred souls. Paul regarded the white deer as a special gift and he thought of him as a protective spirit over West Knob.

They had ridden for over an hour and were returning home when they came to a small stream. Just as Paul's horse was about to enter the water, a black bear, on the other side of the creek, stepped out from the thick undergrowth to the right. When he saw the two horses, he turned and ran deep into the forest. The horse, frightened by the episode, reared up and threw Paul to the ground causing him to strike his head on a rock and it rendered him unconscious. Joseph raced back to the house to get help. Ben, the caretaker, and Charles ran to the scene and stayed with Paul until an emergency helicopter from Edwardton arrived and took Paul to Mercy Hospital.

In the hospital, he remained unaware of his surroundings for almost two weeks. The whole Devon family was continually by his side. When he finally came out of his coma, the doctors gave the family little hope of a complete recovery. It seemed as though the doctors may be right. They suggested putting Paul in a private care facility, but Charles and Rebecca would never ever entertain the thought. If it were to be, Paul would remain behind the gates of West Knob for the rest of his life.

Charles and Rebecca were devastated, as was Joseph. They were determined to provide Paul with the best possible avenue of professional care available. When Paul was finally able to return home from the hospital, the Devon's employed a full-time nurse, plus physical and speech therapists.

As the months went by, Paul's mobility returned to almost normal and his speech continued to improve. Occasionally, he would have episodes of frustration; but when those periods passed, he returned to an almost passive state of mind.

The Devon's now made West Knob their permanent residence. Here Paul would be sheltered from the outside world and surrounded by the family and mountains he loved. Here, they felt, was the best environment for his care. Charles and Rebecca would never give up on Paul. With every improvement in his condition, they felt more and more that they had done the right thing by bringing Paul home. They experienced great joy as Paul passed every obstacle toward his recovery.

Ben Jenkins was the caretaker of the Devon estate and he seemed, without words, to be able to communicate with Paul. When he was with Ben, it produced a calming affect on him. Ben made it a point to see that he and Paul would take short walks in the mountains and let him get reunited with the outdoors he loved.

He had taken care of the grounds and the house at West Knob for years while the Devon's were in Philadelphia. Now Charles asked him if he would consider working for them full-time. He could see the improvement in Paul when Ben was around. Ben had been a widower for many years and enjoyed working for the Devon's. He agreed and moved into the apartment above the carriage house. When he moved in, he brought along his mixed-breed collie, Beau. They had been together for nine years and one would be lost without the other.

Charles and Joseph, who was now working with his father,

commuted to the Philadelphia business every week, returning to West Knob on the weekends. Joseph took on the responsibility of the stores in Philadelphia, New York and Baltimore. He would spend several days a week at the satellite stores and check on the progress of each business. He was a natural promoter and the employees loved to have him in the store.

As the fall turned to winter, Paul continued to improve. Even though he had and an occasional outburst of frustration, to Charles and Rebecca, his recovery so far, had been a miracle.

Before Paul's accident, the family had a steady stream of guests from the city and entertained many of Charles's clients at their mountain retreat. They were friendly with the locals and were known as the Aristocrats of the Mountain. Since the accident though, they were seldom seen and when they did have contact in the community, they seemed distant and impersonal. The people of the village understood their sadness and all they could do for them was to give them moral support. Only time would bring the family back to the way they were. But for now, they were no longer the Devon's everyone had known.

All through the fall and winter, Joseph and his father, commuted back and forth from West Knob to their Philadelphia business. As the months went on, Joseph took on more and more responsibility. The business continued to grow and prosper and it seemed that everything the Devon's touched turned to gold. More craftsmen had to be added to the business to keep up with the growing demand for the fine Devon furniture.

It was January and Joseph was anxious to get back home to West Knob to see Paul. He had spent the week at the Baltimore stores and then returned to Philadelphia. As he left the city, the Payne's gray clouds signaled signs of bad weather. He loved the drive to West Knob and when he was driving, he could organize his thoughts and plans for the coming week.

On his way home this time, he stopped at an antique store and purchased a beautiful bronze inkwell with the head of an owl. Its wings spread downward forming a tray to hold a writing pen. He always brought a gift home for Paul; especially something involved with birds or animals.

As he headed over the mountains and through the valleys toward home, a few snowflakes started to fall. As he approached the last mountain, the snow was starting to stick to the road so he drove slowly up toward the summit. Not only did he have a surprise for Paul but he also had a surprise for his parents. Without warning, a white tail buck jumped in front of his car. He swerved to avoid hitting the deer and as he did, the car on the icy road, went into a spin and slid over the edge of the mountain. When the car stopped rolling at the bottom of the steep slope, Joseph lay unconscious.

When Joseph didn't arrive home as scheduled, his mother became worried. He was never late and he had just phoned her an hour ago to let her know he was on his way and would be home shortly. Charles had come home earlier in the day, but Joseph had some business to take care of at the Philadelphia store and would make the drive later. Rebecca felt she could no longer wait and phoned the Highway Patrol. They assured her that they would do what they could, but the light snowfall had turned into a full-fledged blizzard. It would be impossible to start a search now and they would have to wait until morning.

At daybreak, the officers began their search. They followed the route Joseph would have taken. An hour after they started, they spotted the overturned car he had been driving at the bottom of South Mountain. When they reached the car, there was nothing they could do for him.

When Charles and Rebecca heard the news, they were near collapse and Paul was as devastated as his parents were.

Three days later, Joseph was buried in the family cemetery at West Knob.

The months that followed Joseph's death were excruciating for the family. Charles lost total interest in the Devon Furniture business and against the wishes and pleading of his wife, sold the entire business. He retreated behind the walls of his West Knob fortress and completely withdrew from the outside world.

Paul's accident was tragic enough but losing Joseph was almost inconceivable to him. Rebecca faired a little better and kept up enough strength to care for Paul and Charles.

In less than one year, the dynasty of the Devon's had practically collapsed. If it weren't for Ben Jenkins and the housekeeper taking care of the Devon's everyday needs, they both would have slowly perished.

As the months went on, Charles, in his devastated state of mind, ordered a mausoleum to be built in the family cemetery to honor Joseph.

Day after day Ben would see Charles walk to the cemetery and spend hours at Joseph's grave. It seemed as though the grieving would never end and West Knob would never again be the same.

As winter turned to spring, a shrine to Joseph began. Local stone masons were hired and followed the detailed plans which Charles had drawn up for Joseph's final resting-place. Paul sat with Ben's dog, Beau, and day after day watched the mausoleum grow toward the heavens.

Charles had ordered an array of flowering shrubs to be planted around the building. In front of the granite sanctuary, two large white marble angels had been placed on either side of the entrance door. White rose bushes reached upward toward the feet of the angels. Behind the iron front gate was a heavy, cherry wood door carved with a likeness of Joseph holding a small white deer and at the bottom was inscribed his name, date of birth and death. It was a gift, a very sad gift, from the oldest master carver who had been employed by the Devon Empire. A large steel plate was attached to the back of the mausoleum awaiting the arrival of a stained glass window, which had been ordered from Italy to replace it. A decorative iron fence surrounded the tomb and the walkway of imported marble. Outside of the iron fence, two marble birdbaths with center fountains had been placed. The whole setting was a magnificently beautiful tribute to a beloved son.

It seemed that the whole Devon dynasty was lost in the confines of the Shrine, behind the walls of West Knob. Even Ben had his doubts about the survival of the Devon's.

With the Devon's past year of tragedy and now the two missing women of Mercyville, the people of the village were wondering if they were living under a sign of bad luck and misfortune?

3

The conclave of opinion makers was sitting around the oversized round table when Charles Devon walked in to the store. It had been over six months since his son, Joseph, had been killed in an automobile accident and nine months since Paul's riding accident. No one except Ben and the housekeeper had seen him for months.

Within the same time period, two young women from the Mercyville area had disappeared.

"Good morning, Charles," said Matt Wallace. "How about joining us for coffee? It's been a long time since we've seen you and we've missed your company."

Charles was pale and had lost a lot of weight. The whole village knew about the terrible disasters, which had befallen the Devon family and they were sympathetic toward them.

Charles hesitated at the offer but then walked over to the eternal pot of coffee and poured himself a cup.

No one was sure what to say, but they were saved when Charles opened the conversation.

"It's been a long time, maybe too long. I guess I should have left West Knob before now, but I had no desire to leave. Ben Jenkins talked me into coming off of the mountain with him. He had to pick up lumber to make some repairs to the carriage house. I'm glad it's finally summer. It will be good for Paul to get back out in the mountains. Yesterday, out near the cemetery, we found a newborn fawn. As we started to approach, the mother came charging out of the woods. Seems like all creatures are protective of their young," he said as tears came to his eyes.

Just then, Ben came in to the store.

"I'm ready if you are Charles. I loaded up the truck and picked up a few things the housekeeper had asked for. Women always have to have something to be picked up at the store!" He said with a smile.

Charles got up from the table and waved good-bye.

"Charles, if you need anything at West Knob, you know we're all here to help," said Billy Wilson, the lumber mill foreman. "Just give us a call and we'll be there."

"Thank you, gentlemen. I'll keep that in mind," Charles said, as he and Ben left the store.

The last months had not been good to the Devon's or to Mercyville. It was almost a month since the women had disappeared and still there were no clues to their whereabouts. Sadness clung to the peaceful valley.

"Please put those chairs against the wall. Then pull the blanket chest over to the right. That will give us enough room for the hutch and I can display the china and crystal on the shelves. That should be about it for today, Martin," said Molly Anderson, owner of the antique barn.

"I would appreciate if you could get here early in the morning. With the auction starting at ten o'clock, there are always the early birds looking for a bargain. Thank you for your help, Martin."

The auction at the antique barn was an annual affair to raise money for the Mercyville Volunteer Fire Department. The sale was always advertised far in advance of the event so a large crowd was expected. It wasn't your everyday yard sale. Both dealers and private citizens donated quality items to the sale. With Molly's antique shop the place of the sale, she donated fifty percent of whatever she sold on auction day from the shop to the fire department. Molly always let them hold it at the barn since there was more than sufficient parking space. People from miles around came to the sale. It would be a welcomed relief from the worry of the past months. The all-day event would consist of buying and socializing.

Molly's helper, the thirty-year-old, six-foot-tall Martin Benson lived five miles west of Mercyville in a small cabin. He survived by doing odd jobs around the area. Martin worked periodically for Molly at her antique shop lifting and rearranging her latest acquisitions. In the fall, he picked up a few dollars helping out during the hay harvest. He also cut firewood, from his land, to sell to the locals and the campers in the summer. In the winter, he made enough money for groceries by plowing snow. He was a loner, but a good worker. Most of the people of Mercyville considered him to be rather strange to say the least, but for the most part, it was a live and let live community. No one could prove it, but some people suspected him of poaching. When you drove by his cabin, during the hunting season, he always had a deer strung up. The perimeter of his fenced-off land was plastered with "No Trespassing", "Posted", "Keep Out", "Private Property" and "Beware of Dog" signs. The latter really didn't seem necessary, as he hadn't had a dog; at least no one had seen a dog behind the fortress of signs, for years. Old Red, his mixed hound, died five years ago. Gunshots were heard at night on numerous occasions coming from his land and the town's people figured he was hunting raccoons. On his property there was an old stone springhouse with water running through it. It was in there that the town folks suspected he stored the unlawfully gained fauna but no one had the nerve to question him on the subject. They felt that the farther away from Martin, the better off you were!

He drove a beat up old pick-up truck with a gun rack in it. There never seemed to be a shortage of arms in the rack behind his head. On the few rare occasions that he came in to the country store, he looked rather shabby, needed a good bath and hadn't washed his clothes recently. His long brown hair hung over the collar of his faded shirt. He had been wearing the same tattered red jacket and coveralls for years. The only time his wardrobe changed was during hunting season when he always bought a brand new fluorescent orange hat. Behind his back, a few smart aleck young men of Mercyville called him 'Stay-away-Martin.'

Molly was right. The early birds started coming at seven-thirty. Martin had arrived around seven and was putting up the folding chairs for the auction. It appeared that Martin had improved his appearance for the auction. Although they were wrinkled, his pants and shirt were clean and it appeared as though he had cut and washed his hair.

Food vendors had pulled over near a group of oak trees and set up tables with red-checked vinyl coverings. The pretzel man, who frequented every public gathering in the county, was preparing stacks of large, soft pretzels in anticipation of a busy day. A few of the early birds found their way to a coffee/donut vendor and took advantage of the folding chairs. Near the barn, Alison and Matt Wallace set up a small booth selling miniature paintings of the Endless Mountains. Fifty percent of the proceeds would go to the fire department.

A large van from Paceton pulled in near the barn. Two men started unloading a large pie cupboard with a tin front and a weathered Amish-blue dry sink. A number of antique dealers from as far away as Lancaster had donated many of the sale items. Families from Lancaster had second-home cabins in the Endless Mountains and were glad to support the Volunteer Fire Department function.

A bed, marble-top wash stand and a huge bureau came next. Martin walked over and helped the men unload the latter items. The beautiful set of walnut bedroom furniture was placed next to the auctioneer's podium.

Molly was busy adding last minute donations to the display tables. There was a lovely white pitcher and bowl set. A twelve-place setting set of China with a gold pattern was unpacked. The china was placed on a beautiful Devon cherry dining room table. The Devon's always made a contribution to the auction but this year the table was among one of the finest items at the auction.

Not everything was an antique. The Quilting Society of Mercyville had donated four beautiful, handmade quilts. A local candlemaker contributed a large crystal bowl filled with handmade wax fruits and berries. The work was so well done that it appeared to be real. The lavish candle display was expected to bring over one hundred dollars. It was really a shame to burn the candle with all of the work that went into it so the candle maker placed a separated small glass candle holder in the very center of the wax fruit so that the main design could still be appreciated as it burned.

Several stores from Edwardton donated some very nice utilitarian items. A microwave, set of twelve crystal glasses, three-figure gift certificates and a stunning reproduction hanging Tiffany lamp were among the many donations.

By the looks of this year's donations, a nice sum of money would be going to the department, Molly thought.

It was a beautiful day in the Endless Mountains. A large crowd of people was expected to attend the auction. Throughout the day, the speculation of the whereabouts of the missing women would dominate the conversation.

Jerry Zimmerman, the auctioneer, drove up and parked behind the barn. He walked around and looked at all of the donated items, making notes as he passed by each auction lot.

The crowds started flocking in for the auction. Some brought trucks or trailers in anticipation of a purchase. The aroma of freshly brewed coffee and deep-fried donuts floated through the air.

It was almost time for the sale to begin and each participant, who planned to bid, had signed up for a bidding number.

The folding chairs were quickly filling up as Jerry took his spot at the podium. Every year, He donated his services for the auction.

The smaller items were auctioned off first. Novelty glassware, antique clothes, dresser sets, stoneware, antique kitchen paraphernalia, braided rugs and several lots of sought after collectibles went first. A set of ten flow-blue plates brought the most money of the lot.

It was almost twelve o'clock when the first lot of items was finished. Jerry took a twenty-minute refreshment break. People waiting for the furniture were getting anxious for it to be put up on the block. Many of the regulars at outdoor auctions brought along their own lawn chairs. They had learned from past experience, that long auctions required creature comforts and getting off of your feet was part of that scenario. Getting what they bid on was next.

The hammer hit the podium and the auction resumed.

First the walnut bedroom set was on the block. Bidding started at a low one thousand dollars. Back and forth bidding numbers were flashed in the air as the price skyrocketed upward. Four individuals were neck and neck as the bidding war continued. At four thousand dollars, the first bidder dropped out of contention. Each of the remaining three pushed the pricing fight to gain control. Finally at five thousand dollars, a second bidder dropped out. The bid went to six thousand dollars. Now, the remaining two hesitated waiting for the other to stop the battle. Reluctantly, the third bidder decided to stop at six thousand, five-hundred dollars. Mary Ellen Weatherstone, the owner of a lovely Bed and Breakfast, was now the proud owner of the polished walnut treasure. At the end of the bidding, a round of applause went throughout the crowd for the fighting foursome of bidders.

Mary Ellen and her husband, Chris, brought a pickup truck and padding to the sale in anticipation of a purchase. Martin helped Chris load the treasure into the back of the truck. She was thrilled at the purchase and knew exactly where she was going to use it. The fire department members were even more pleased.

As the battle for the various goods continued, a car pulled up in the back of the crowd near the road. It was Ben Jenkins, Charles and Rebecca Devon and their son Paul.

Charles had only been seen once in the last six months. For the first time in months, his wife and son were out of the confines of West Knob.

Rebecca and Paul unfolded their lawn chairs while Charles and Ben looked over a table with antique toys. There was an iron horse and an iron deer of 1900 vintages. Both had their original paint and boxes. Charles asked Ben to get a bidding card and bid for him on both of the metal animals, no matter how high the bidding went. Charles wanted them for Paul and for him, money was no object.

Charles went back and stood next to the seated Rebecca and Paul. Paul looked well for all he had gone through. His walking was almost normal. The outbursts of frustration that came after the accidents had stopped. To outsiders, Paul looked perfectly normal. His recovery, to this point was just short of a miracle.

In a few minutes the bids were opened for the antique fauna. A toy dealer was there and wanted the iron relics. He was prepared to pay just about any price, but he didn't know he would be bidding against Charles Devon. To the shock of the dealer, the price started unbelievably high. Very soon Ben had secured the iron horse and deer for Paul's collection.

No one had seen the next item coming to the block. Martin carried the covered form out of the barn. When he took the cover off, there was an exquisite, mint condition, antique carousel horse. Oh's and Ah's swept through the crowd.

Charles Devon walked up to the front where Ben was standing. He whispered something in Ben's ear and returned to his family in the back row.

Even Jerry, the auctioneer, was surprised at the treasure. He opened the bidding at one thousand dollars. Back and forth the bids were raised by a thousand dollars at a time. Finally, a dealer raised the bid to nine thousand dollars. He was sure the treasure was to going to be his. Ben raised the bid to ten thousand dollars and with that, the carousel horse had found a new home at West Knob.

Ben carried the wooden horse back to Charles, as Martin glared at the head of the Devon dynasty.

Martin hated Charles Devon. Charles had caught Martin poaching at West Knob. He confiscated the deer he had shot and threatened to turn him over to the game warden if he ever set foot again on his property. That was over a year ago, but Martin vowed he would someday get even with the Devon's. Money wouldn't stop Martin from getting revenge. Martin was a mountain man and he didn't need much money. The mountains were his subsistence. He felt that the mountains were his to do with as he liked, as long as no one was harmed, and no Devon or anyone else would stand in his way.

The Volunteer Fire Department Auction had come to a close. People were packing their trucks and trailers with their newly-acquired treasures and were getting ready to head home.

Martin stayed and put the folding chairs back in the barn. It was getting late and everyone was tired. Tomorrow he would come back and clean up the grounds. The Barbecue Chicken man offered Martin the leftover chickens. At least tonight, dinner would be a change from the regular diet of venison and an occasional trout.

Driving back to his cabin, Martin thought about Charles Devon. It was time to get even with him; time to take back His Mountains.

The McCartys and Vermillions had pooled their resources and hired a new private detective from Baltimore. They weren't going to stop searching until they found their daughters; dead or alive.

As Jason Rowe, the private detective from Baltimore, drove north up Interstate Fifteen, he tried to make sense of what he had been told about the women's disappearance. Whoever had kidnapped them could have taken their cars and money, yet neither was touched. Both of the women were taken from approximately the same isolated strip of road. His first thought was that it had to be someone familiar with the area; someone living close by, but why?

It was noon when he pulled up in front of the Weatherstone's Bed and Breakfast. Mary Ellen had been expecting him and showed him to his room on the second floor. From the window he could see out across the Mercyville valley. Setting high on a plateau he could see a mansion and wondered who it belonged to. When he had unpacked, he went downstairs.

"We're in the kitchen. Come join us for coffee," Mary Ellen called.

As he sipped his coffee, he asked about the mansion. "I was wondering who owned that house out on the plateau?"

Mary Ellen filled him in on all of the particulars of the estate and the Devon family; including Joseph's death and Paul's accident.

"Now that you mentioned it, I remember hearing about the Devon furniture stores in Baltimore. They are very expensive stores, but I understand that the furniture is beautiful. The prices are out of my league but I have a friend who wouldn't buy anything but Devon furniture. He said he wouldn't have anything else, even if it were given to him. It seemed a small world being near the Devon estate. I wasn't aware that they lived up here," Jason said. "I think I will go down to the country store and see if I can come up with anything new. I would also like to go out to where they found the cars and look around. Thanks again for the coffee. I'll see you this evening."

Just as Jason Rowe was going in to the country store, a big man came out at the same time and bumped into him. It was Martin Benson. The slight collision caused Martin to drop his groceries.

"I'm sorry," Jason said. "Let me help you pick up these things"

As Martin leaned over to retrieve his groceries, a small gold bracelet with a gold robin charm fell out of his pocket. He quickly threw it in the bag with his purchases. He never said a word to Jason and just left the store in a hurry.

Jason thought the man was odd but maybe he was just in a hurry. He was here to do a job and he wasn't leaving until the job was done.

Three of the opinion makers were sitting at the over-sized round table sipping coffee. Jason walked over to the men, introduced himself and explained why he was there. None of the men could offer any information on the missing women.

"As I was coming in the store, I accidentally bumped into a big man going out. He seemed to be in a big hurry. Do you know who he is?" Jason asked.

"That is Martin Benson. He has a small cabin about four or five miles west of here. He doesn't come to town very often. Nobody really knows too much about him. He keeps pretty much to himself. Pointing in a westerly direction, Matt Wallace directed Jason in the area of Martin's homestead. "You'll know it when you get there," he said. "It's all fenced in and about every ten feet or so, you will see some kind of warning sign! Everybody stays away from Martin mainly because he just doesn't seem to want to associate with anyone. He's kind of a strange duck. The police questioned him, as they did everyone else around here, but he didn't know anything about the disappearances. In that respect, he was like everyone else in Mercyville. Both cars of the missing women were found along the road out near his place. That's about all anyone knows."

"I'm staying at the Weatherstone's Bed and Breakfast. If you should think of anything relevant to the case, I would appreciate a call," Jason said, as he turned to leave.

Jason was going to meet with the McCartys and the Vermillions in the evening. Rather than burn daylight, he decided to drive out toward Benson's cabin. He wanted to get a feel of the country so he might as well start there.

Driving west, from the country store/post office, he understood why people loved the Endless Mountains. It was so peaceful and quiet, unlike the congestion of Baltimore. He knew he was here on business, but to the city man it seemed more like a vacation.

As he reached the top of the mountain, he had a perfect view of the Devon estate on the right. A mile down the road, on the left, he knew he was in the vicinity of Martin's place. It wasn't hard to define the property lines. On his fence was every kind everyone kind of sign that the Edwardton hardware store had in stock! Halfway down the fence line was a gate covered with No Trespassing signs. The lane behind the gate led to a small cabin with an old pickup truck sitting next to it. There was no sign of Martin.

Jason continued to drive westward and when he came to the end of the fence decorated with the not-so-welcome signs he knew he was at the beginning of Martin's property. He pulled off of the road into a small clearing and got out of his car.

On the opposite side of the road, across from the fence, he started walking back from where he had just driven. He was searching for anything...any small clue that would connect to the missing women. He had walked about a half mile, pushing aside the leaves on the ground with his foot. There had to be something, he thought. But so far he had found nothing. Then he turned around and started retracing his footsteps back to the car. Out of the corner of his eye, he thought he saw someone watching him, but when he glanced to the right, he saw only the silhouettes of two deer. He continued walking back toward his car. As he looked ahead a shiny object on the edge of the road caught his eye. When he picked it up, he could see it was a small gold bird's nest. He turned it over and over in his hand and then put it in his pocket. This was the second gold object he had seen in the last two hours. He thought it was a coincidence or was it?

Even though it was June, it started to cool off as the sun went down over the mountains. The sky changed from a brilliant cerulean to shades of orange, yellow and lavender. The deep blue lines of the mountains were silhouetted against the rainbow of hues. Jason wasn't sure why, but he felt that this had been a good day.

Mary Ellen Weatherstone had told him about the local recreation ground and the availability of their small restaurant area. He had no choice of restaurants in Mercyville. The recreation ground was it for the evening.

Driving up the road to the recreation ground store he saw dozens of parked campers; second homes on wheels.

As he entered the store, he saw that several Highway Department men had stopped for coffee before heading home. Jason had read the menu on the chalkboard and decided on a pizza. He hadn't had much to eat today, so pizza sounded good.

As he was eating, a man and a woman came rushing in the front door.

"We were in Edwardton today shopping and when we got home to our camper, the door was ripped off. We discovered that damn bear had made himself at home again. The floor was covered with food and he had gotten into the refrigerator. A gallon of milk was spilled everywhere! Well, it's just one damn mess again! He left a trail of crackers going back into the woods. I'm sick and tired of this! This is the second time in a month that bear partied at my house! I hope someone gets him this bear season!" Frank Duckworth yelled. "I finally talked my wife into living at the recreation ground for the summer and now that bear is ruining the whole damn thing. She's getting too scared to be here. In season or out of season, the next time he comes around we're all going to have bear stew! I've had all I can take! I retired here for a little peace and quiet and all I get is that damn bear."

"I'll call the game warden and have him check on your damage. I am sure when we tell him what the bear's been doing; they will probably relocate him to another county far away from here," Evelyn Mueller, a worker at the store, said. "That bear has been causing too much trouble lately and I think he better go before someone gets hurt. He's always getting into the Dumpster at night and what a mess in the morning!"

Well, thought Jason, things aren't really that dull in Mercyville after all!

4

Jason Rowe walked up the steps of the white, two-story Victorian house and knocked on the door. A lady with blond hair and crystal-blue eyes answered.

"Good evening. I'm Jason Rowe," he said.

"Come in. We've been expecting you. I'm Sarah McCarty, Mary's mother," the lady replied.

As he entered the living room, Sarah introduced him to Karen and Bill Kline, Leslie Vermillion's parents and Sam Vermillion, her husband. Then she introduced him to her husband, Allan.

"I'm here to find out what you know, if anything, about your daughters' disappearance," Jason said.

Allan was the first to speak up. "We know very little, in fact the police have told us they know absolutely nothing. They feel our daughters were taken out of the county. It's crazy! Both incidents are just insane! We can't eat, we can't sleep! Not knowing whether they are dead or alive is driving us over the edge. It's on your mind twenty-four hours a day. Somewhere there has to be an explanation. Mary and Leslie were both very responsible individuals. We feel something or someone made them stop on the road. Neither one of them would have picked up anyone they didn't know, so that is out of the question. It's been four weeks since Mary disappeared and the same since Leslie vanished. We need help now and we need answers. Not knowing anything is the worst of all," he said.

"We feel the girls are still alive. I guess it's just hope, but that's how we feel. Practically every cabin has been searched, including many of the out buildings. Police brought in search dogs when each of the girls disappeared; but, they didn't find anything either. We're at our wits end," Bill Kline said.

"I understand how your must feel. I'll do whatever I can to get to the bottom of this and I'm not leaving Mercyville until I have some answers," Jason said.

He reached in his pocket and pulled out the tiny gold bird's nest. "Do any of you recognize this?" Jason asked, as he passed the tiny gold bird's nest around the room.

When Sarah McCarty looked at it, she said, "I think that I may have seen something like that, but I can't remember where or when. My mind has been so cluttered since Mary disappeared that I can hardly make it through a day."

"Don't worry about it, Sarah. If anything comes to mind, you know where you can reach me. Tomorrow, I'm going to see the police and then I'm going to look around Mercyville. There has to be someone who knows something and maybe it's such a minor clue that they don't even realize that it may be important," Jason said.

As Jason got up to leave, Sam Vermillion walked him to the door. "Everyone has my number. I'm staying at Weatherstone's Bed and Breakfast and if you think of anything, you can reach me there in the morning or evening. I know it's hard not to worry, but I have a feeling we'll get to the bottom of this soon."

Paul Devon's recovery was moving forward. With the help of the speech therapist, his language skills had continued to improve. The doctors were amazed at his progress. Six months ago they gave the Devons very little hope of any recovery, but then, doctors aren't always right. The Devons felt that a higher being had taken charge of Paul's care.

He was now able to go for longer walks in the mountains. Ben's dog, Beau, usually accompanied Paul on his outings. The dog seemed to know Paul needed him so he always stayed close beside him when they walked through the woods. When Beau was walking with Ben, he felt free to run off and chase an occasional rabbit, but not when he was with Paul.

It was ten o'clock when Paul and Beau headed out for their daily excursion. The sun filtered down through the towering hemlocks and was drying the morning dew off of the thick undergrowth. The woods opened up to a large clearing that held the Devon family cemetery. Paul stopped in front of Joseph's mausoleum and a sudden sadness crept over him. Beau walked around the iron fence and began frantically sniffing the ground. The mist on one of the marble angels streaked down her cheek giving her the appearance of tears. Paul's eyes filled with a care only a brother could feel as he continued walking across the clearance and into the woods.

They had walked a quarter of a mile, when Paul thought he heard branches cracking in the thick brush to his right. Beau started barking and headed in the direction of the sound. Paul surmised that it was a white tail deer. As he strained to look through the filtering sunlight, he thought he saw a figure running away from him. Beau must have seen the moving form and started running after it. Paul went after Beau and called for him to come back. Reluctantly, the dog returned to Paul. He turned and headed back through the woods, past the mausoleum and toward the house. The morning walk had been unsettling to Paul. When he reached the house, Rebecca was outside planting flowers.

"That was a short walk," she said. "I thought you and Beau would be gone longer. Beau seems a little agitated."

He struggled to find the right words about seeing the figure in the woods.

"Paul, are you trying to tell me you saw someone in the woods?" his mother asked.

He nodded his head, yes.

"Is that why Beau is so excited?"

"Yes," Paul said.

"I think I had better tell Ben and your father about this. This is making me very uncomfortable," Rebecca said.

When the men came in for lunch, Rebecca related Paul's incident on his walk in the woods.

Charles was disturbed about what he heard.

"I'll take Beau this afternoon and go out and look around," Ben said. "After the disappearance of those young women, every strange thing that happens is suspect."

As they finished lunch, Ben got up and left with Beau following close behind.

Jason received a call from Sarah the next day. "Hello, Jason. This is Sarah McCarty. You said to call if I remembered anything. I think I did see that gold bird nest before and I believe Mary had one similar to that one. It was on a gold bracelet with a gold bird on it. As I recall, she bought it from a jewelry maker at a craft show in Edwardton. I haven't seen it for years," she said.

"Thank you, Sarah. I appreciate the call. I'll get back with you soon," Jason said.

Jason remembered the incident at the country store/post office with Martin Benson, particularly the gold bracelet. Could Martin be involved in the women's disappearance? he thought. He decided to talk to Martin. He thought it was odd that he would have that bracelet and out of character for a mountain man like Martin to have a woman's gold bracelet.

As Jason drove up to Martin's place, he saw him out front chopping wood. Martin didn't seem too thrilled at having a visitor, especially when he was working. He certainly didn't throw out the red carpet and would never have received an award for hospitality.

Jason got out of the car and walked over to the gate, making sure he stayed on the outside perimeter. "Hello, I'm Jason Rowe. I'd like to talk to you about the missing McCarty and Vermillion women," he said.

"I know who you are. I remember you from the store," Martin called over the gate. "I don't know nothing about them women. I told the police that and I'm telling you the same thing. I don't need nobody else out here snooping around!"

"I just have one question to ask you. When I ran into you at the store, you dropped a gold bracelet with a bird on it. Do you still have that bracelet?" Jason asked.

"I don't think that's any of your business whether I have it or not! I didn't steal it. I found it. What I find, I keep," Martin said, agitated.

Getting Martin ticked off was the last thing Jason wanted to happen. "I don't want the bracelet," he said, and reached into his pocket, pulling out the small gold bird nest. He reached over the fence and handed it to Martin. "I just wanted to see if the bracelet you found and the bird's nest go together."

For the first time, Martin seemed to let down his guard. He examined the small gold object in his hand, then gave it back to Jason. "Wait here," he growled, and turned heading back to his cabin.

As Jason waited outside of the gate he studied the display of signs on both the fence and the gate. No, thought Jason, Martin wasn't a member of any hospitality committee and for his own safety, he wasn't going to cross over the gate.

In a few minutes, Martin returned with the bracelet and handed it to Jason. A small link on the bracelet was broken and he could see that the bird's nest was a perfect fit.

"Can I ask you where you found it?" Jason asked.

"You ask a lot of questions. What do you want to know for? It's mine. I told you I found it and what I find, I keep," Martin said in a very gruff voice.

"Martin, I think this bracelet may have belonged to Mary McCarty, one of the missing women. Her mother remembered Mary having one similar to it," Jason said, and handed the bracelet back to Martin.

Martin thought for a moment and looked up the road. He pointed to a downed birch tree near the side of the road. "I found it over there near that birch…right on the edge of the road." He reiterated, in no uncertain terms, that he didn't steal the bracelet — that he found it.

"Martin, there's just one other thing. Did you see or hear anything around the time the women disappeared…anything at all?" Jason asked.

"No! I don't concern myself with things that ain't none of my of business," he said. He turned and started to walk away. "Wait," he said. "There was one thing, but I guess it's not important. Both days them women disappeared, I remember hearing somebody revving up a truck. I know it was a truck because it sounded just like my other truck that I had. It had the same sound. I remember it for sure. I was hunting rabbits and just ready to shoot when that damn noise scared the rabbit. The second time I heard the same noise I was down at the springhouse. I thought it was probably some town kids showing off their trucks. Now that's all I know so don't be in a hurry to come back here either. I got things to do!" With that said, Martin walked back to the woodpile and started to resume his cutting.

"Martin," Jason called. "Did you tell the police about hearing the truck?"

"Why would I tell them that? I just remembered it now. Anyway, what could they tell by a truck revving up?" he said.

The whole thing is strange, thought Jason, as he drove back to town. Did Martin really find the bracelet? Was he hiding something? He wanted to search Martin's place, but with his attitude toward outsiders, it didn't seem likely that would happen anytime soon. Anyway, it would be chancy at best that he'd let anyone near his place...well, maybe the police would have better odds at looking around. Only time will tell.

5

Martin Benson wasn't the only one who hated Charles Devon. The Aaron brothers were pretty close behind Martin. Both of the brothers were over six-feet tall with dark hair and it was obvious that they belonged to the teeth-optional club.

They had a fairly large hunting cabin about a half a mile from the Devon estate and their land connected with the Devons' land. During hunting season, they made part of their living as guides and the rest of the year they logged. Before Charles Devon arrived on the scene, the Aarons took their hunters on the estate land. Charles put a stop to that. To him, riding trails were more important than hunting. The logging business was getting more and more competitive and nobody was really making any money to speak of. The Aarons were tired of being broke. They needed money and they didn't care how they got it. They wanted out of Mercyville and the sooner the better.

"If it weren't for your brilliant idea, we would have been out of here weeks ago. Now we're in a hell of a mess and I didn't bargain for murder! That wasn't in our plan! Getting those two women…getting the ransom money…that was it! I'm getting tired of having those women here! We're going to have to get rid of them, but I'm not going to kill them. If we're going to make our move, it better be soon. Like you said, all we need is that Devon kid then the whole damn town can soak. With Paul Devon, the ante is up! I saw him this morning and I could have had him then, but he had a dog with him and I was lucky to get away. I'll give it two more days, then that's it; I'm out of here…money or not! But I'm telling you again, I ain't gonna be part of any murder. If you want them dead, you kill them yourself…I'm not. We never planned on keeping the women this long and we never planned on killing them. The whole mess is getting on my nerves. I see that Devon kid walking everyday. Tomorrow, I'm going back the estate and if I see the kid, it's all over. He's mine. If he has that damn dog again, I'll shoot him," Rich Aaron said to his brother, Tom.

When the Aaron brothers kidnapped the women, they planned on holding the whole village of Mercyville hostage for the ransom. But Tom had a sudden brainstorm and now they had to change their plans because town money wasn't good enough for him. If they had the Devon kid the whole picture would change. The Devons had big money…and big money was what they needed.

From the day the women were kidnapped, the women had never seen their captors. The men always wore ski masks when they were around their hostages. The women were never left alone as one or the other brother was always downstairs.

Mary McCarty and Leslie Vermillion were in the loft of the Aaron's cabin. In the large open loft, there was a bed at either end. The brothers had handcuffed them to the beds. From where Mary was held, she could see the Devon mansion out of the dormer window and from Leslie's view; she could see the main road through Mercyville toward Edwardton. They were so close to home, but it didn't feel like it.

When the police were searching the area Leslie could see their cars going up and down the road and search dogs heading in to the woods.

"Mary," Leslie whispered, so the brothers couldn't hear her. "I don't think I can stand this any more. We have to get out of here. Our families must be frantic with worry. If they only knew how close we were to them."

The days weren't as bad as the nights. With no lights in the loft, it was pitch dark at night. The only lights are the headlights of cars flashing on the wall when they go by.

The downstairs door opened and light crept up in to the loft. Tom Aaron was coming up the steps.

"Here's your meal. Enjoy it! It may be your last," he said. He put the tray with the food on the floor and his flashlight on the table next to Mary as he released her right wrist.

"When are you going to let us go? We haven't done anything to you. Why are you doing this?" Mary demanded .

"Shut up and eat your food. You're lucky you even have food and you're damn lucky you're still alive," he said.

Tom walked across the room to Leslie's bed and took off one of her handcuffs. "Here's your last supper," he said with a smirk on his face. "It won't be long and I won't have to feed you two any more." He turned and went back downstairs. As he closed the door, darkness fell across the room once again.

The two women were afraid to talk. They knew that he sometimes listened at the bottom of the stairs. They struggled to eat in the dark. Even though they weren't hungry, both knew that they had to keep up their strength if they were to survive this ordeal. Downstairs the men planned their last and hopefully their final move. Tomorrow they would get the Devon kid and it shouldn't be too hard they thought. Since the kid's accident, they didn't think he could be all there in the head.

"We'll go over in the morning and wait for him to come out for his walk, and then we'll grab him. After that, all we have to do is wait for the money. I'll leave the ransom note on that shrine they built. I'll have them put the money at the back door of the Mercyville Church. They'll do it if they ever want to see that kid and those women again," Tom said.

Ben Jenkins, with his dog Beau, had searched the whole Devon estate including the area where Paul thought he saw someone. Ben had found nothing he considered suspicious and was sure it must have been a deer. He went back to the house and reported his findings to Charles.

"Thanks a lot, Ben," Charles said. "Ever since the women disappeared, Rebecca gets a little nervous at every little thing. The least little noise she hears at night, I have to get up and check it out.

This house is pretty old and a few creaks come with age. It's just like people, the older you get, the more creaks you have."

"I finished all of the repairs to the carriage house and everything is in pretty good shape now. I'm going out and linseed oil the door at the mausoleum and I want to clean the birdbaths too. If you need anything else done, just let me know." Ben said

Beau followed Ben out to the cemetery. He was really too tired from the morning hike around the estate but where Ben went, Beau was close behind.

Ben unlocked the iron grill, took the rags and linseed oil and wiped over the cherry carved door. The stunning carving of Joseph with the small deer in his hand brought thoughts of happier times. Ben had known him since he was born and he thought that he was a wonderful, caring and talented person and it didn't seem fair that he was taken from life so young.

Beau was so exhausted, he just lay on the marble walkway and watched the finches landing and taking off from the birdbaths. Simultaneously, Ben and Beau heard a branch crack in the woods. Beau's ears went up as Ben turned toward the sound. A white tail deer jumped over a fallen tree with a fawn close by its side. That's probably what Paul heard yesterday, he thought.

When he got back to the house, he could see Charles in the driveway talking to a stranger. He walked over to the men and Charles introduced Ben to Jason Rowe, the private detective from Baltimore.

"Ben, Jason wanted to know if we had heard or had seen anything that was suspicious about the time the women disappeared? I already told him we had talked to the police and we didn't know anything. Do you have anything to add?" Charles asked.

I can't think of a thing. The only strange thing that has happened up here was yesterday. When Paul was out for a walk, he thought he saw something out past the cemetery in the woods. I checked everything this morning and all I saw were deer and at the far end, to the north, I saw a few wild turkeys. That's about all I can add," Ben said.

"Did either of you gentlemen ever hear anyone driving around and revving up the engine? It sounds strange, but I thought I'd ask," Jason said.

"I can't say I have," Ben said. "But, then, I never really thought about it."

"Well, if you folks hear or see anything out of the ordinary, give me a call. I'm staying at the Weatherstone's Bed and Breakfast. If I'm not there, Mary Ellen will take the message and I'll get back to you," Jason said. "Thanks again." He got in his car and left.

Jason couldn't believe he had met Charles Devon. He was such a nice man, especially considering all he has been through lately, he thought.

Don't be so damn stupid, Rich! We can't bring him here! We have enough headaches with them women! They don't know who we are. They've never seen us and bringing that Devon kid here is out of the question!" Tom screamed.

"Well, what do you plan on doing with him...put him in the middle of town with a sign tied to him saying, 'We want money?'" Rich said, sarcastically.

"Shut up and listen!" Tom said. "As soon as he is missing, the whole town will be crawling with cops. They'll be tearing every house, barn, shed and cabin apart from top to bottom. The hills will be crawling with them, and where do you think they won't be checking?"

"I don't know where...probably in the house," Rich said in a disgusted tone.

"Don't be so damn dumb! That's the first place they'll look. They always look in the house and around the property," Tom said, staring at Rich in disbelief!

"Well, where, for God's sake, where?" Rich asked, panicked.

"If you'll calm down, I'll tell you where! We put him in that monument to his brother. I was over in the woods one day when they were building the place. They have a heavy, steel plate bolted to the back of that tomb. On the front they have a wooden door with an iron grill over it. When you take off the steel plate, the hole is big enough to climb through. We drug the kid, tape his mouth shut and tie him up.

We put him in the building so he can keep his brother company! They'll never think of looking in there. He'll be right under their nose and they won't even know it. If they do find him, we'll be long gone.

"Tonight we go over there and loosen all of the bolts on the back of the plate and that way we won't waste time in the morning. The faster we get out there the better. After we get him in that vault, we'll seal it back up then we'll leave the ransom note on the iron grill in front of the door and we're out of there. Then it's only a matter of time and we're on our way to sunny Florida. No more damn cold winters and no more scratching to make a few dollars. It's our turn Rich, and we're not going to be poor any more. Now get the wrenches and we'll get out of here," Tom said.

"What about the women?" Rich asked.

"They'll be all right," Tom said. "Just turn up the radio and they won't even know we are gone. Get those ski masks and let's get this thing done."

The Aaron brothers crept through the woods like two black moles. They knew the woods like the back of their hand. Since they were kids, they lived in the mountains and the forest was their second home.

The half-full moon made it easier to find their way through the hemlocks and thick underbrush. Tom held up his hand to signal to stop. There was something moving through the bushes about one hundred feet ahead of them.

"Oh, my God!" Tom whispered. "It's a bear! The damn thing is huge! It must be the one that has been getting in the recreation ground Dumpster. Don't move! We don't need any more headaches than we already have."

The bear raised up on his hind legs and sniffed the air as he looked in the direction of the two brothers. Their hearts were pounding so hard, almost audible in the still forest. As they watched the bear, it went back down on all fours and turned away from the direction of the men. It walked slowly through the small clearing and back into the thick underbrush.

The men stayed frozen in place for a long time. When Tom thought it was safe, he signaled Rich to move ahead. As they approached the cemetery, they could see lights from the mansion an eighth of a mile away. Moonlight bounced off of the family headstones and the mausoleum stood like a giant guard watching over the sleeping Devons of the past.

Slowly, they moved through the trees until they were behind the Shrine.

"Give me a wrench. I'll start on this side and you start on the other side," Rich said.

The men worked slowly as not to make any noise. They had loosened the heavy bolts holding the steel plate. They left them on just loose enough so that they could get them off easily in the morning. After a half-hour, the deed was done. As they were about to leave, Rich dropped the heavy wrench on the marble walkway and the sound vibrated through the quiet night. They didn't move for fear someone may have heard the noise.

"Pick up the wrench and let's get out of here. We're not finished yet," Tom whispered.

They crept slowly back through the trees and over the hill to their cabin. As they got close, they could hear the radio they had left on. When they went inside, Rich went upstairs to check on the women and found that they were both asleep. When he came back downstairs, Tom was cutting letters and words out of the newspapers and old hunting magazines.

"I'm not about to have them trace anything to us. I'm glueing this note together. They won't know who did it and besides that everyone will be too frantic looking for them women and that Devon kid!" Tom said.

When Tom had finished, Rich read the note, "If you want your son and the women back put one million dollars in a box. Leave it behind the Mercyville Church at the back door at 3:00 a.m., Wednesday morning. Try to follow, and they are all going to be dead."

Now all they needed was daylight. They had what the town wanted most and the town had what they needed the most.

Ben Jenkins couldn't sleep so he made himself a cup of coffee and went out on the deck of the apartment above the carriage house. Beau was already asleep on the deck in his favorite spot.

The moon was half-full and silhouetted the mansion against the sky. It was an eerily quiet night in Mercyville. From the deck, Ben could see five or six deer come out of the woods and graze on the lawn. One went over to Rebecca's newly planted flowerbed and was munching on the young plants. He didn't think she would be too happy when she saw what that deer had done.

He looked across the hills and realized how peaceful everything was at West Knob. When he looked out to his left, he saw a flash of light. It flashed on and off for five or six minutes. He had never seen a light coming from that direction and wondered what it was. He decided it could wait until morning, and went back to bed.

"Get up Rich.' It's time to go. Today is the day we get that Devon kid and today is the day we get our share of the Devons' cash," Tom said.

They got dressed just as the sun was coming through the cabin window.

"It's a little early, isn't it?" Rich moaned.

"No. We're going to get out of here early and go sit and wait. It's never too early to get your share of the world and Brother, ours is out there waiting for us. We were too dumb to realize that we could have done this a long time ago. Get those masks and don't forget the needle. Bring one of those guns too, we may need it," Tom said.

The two men, dressed in camouflage and ski masks, made their way through the thick underbrush and heavy foliage. It was still early and heavy dew covered everything. They took cover in the trees behind the mausoleum and waited for their unsuspecting prey.

Back at the mansion, the Devon family was just finishing breakfast. "Paul," his father said. "I don't think you have to worry about anyone being around here. Ben searched everywhere yesterday with Beau and he didn't see anything out of the ordinary...only deer and a few wild turkeys. When you go out, just take Beau with you and you'll be fine. He's the best protection you could have.

"I'm going to ride along to town with Ben. He has to pick up a part for the mower and we won't be too long."

The speech therapist would be coming at eleven o'clock so Paul thought he would take his walk a little early. As he went out the kitchen door, he nearly fell over Beau who was lying on the top step waiting for him.

"Let's go," Paul said to the eager dog. They couldn't be gone too long today.

As Paul walked on the pathway to the cemetery, he had an uneasy feeling. He knew that his father was probably right and the only thing he had seen yesterday was probably a deer.

Beau ran a short bit ahead searching for something to chase. When he came to the cemetery, his nose went down to the ground. He ran all around the shrine at a serious pace, then continued toward the woods on the path in front of him.

Paul was just coming out of the woods into the resting place of the Devons. Just when he was in front of the mausoleum, two camouflaged men with hoods attacked him from each side.

Tom pushed Paul to the ground as Rich reached for the needle. Beau, who had run a little ahead, turned back when he heard the commotion and saw Paul on the ground. In a flash, he ran back and leaped through the air at Rich's throat and knocked him off balance. The shock of the dog caused him to fall over onto the marble walkway. He kept hitting the dog to get him off, but Beau held fast. He finally got one hand free and fumbled for a rock near his head. Grabbing the rock in his right hand, he smashed the canine over the head. Beau went limp and just lay there.

Tom was still struggling with Paul as Rich pulled the syringe out of his pocket and jabbed it into his arm. In a few seconds, he was unconscious and the two men pulled him behind the mausoleum. They taped his mouth shut and as Tom tied him up, Rich took the bolts off of the steel slab. He leaned it against the wall and for the first time since Joseph was laid to rest, sunlight filtered into the sacred tomb. They lifted the unconscious man through the hole in the back of the mausoleum and laid him in the corner.

"Hurry up and let's get out of here," Tom said.

They put the slab back in place and secured the bolts. When they were finished Tom put the ransom note on the iron grill in front of the cherry, carved door, then they headed back out through the woods.

"I think I killed that dog," Rich said.

"That's the least of our problems. I should have killed the kid too, but who's going to pay for a corpse?" Tom asked.

When they reached the cabin, Tom pulled off his mask and went inside. With his mask still on, Rich went upstairs to check on the women. He uncuffed Mary and led her to the bathroom.

"Hurry up, I don't have all day!" Rich shouted through the door.

When Mary came out of the bathroom, he handcuffed her back to the bed. Then he let Leslie up. When she was finished, he shoved her back to the bed and handcuffed her again.

"You don't think you're going to get away with this? The whole town is looking for us," Leslie screamed.

He pulled back his hand to hit her, but had second thoughts. We don't need any damaged merchandise at this point. One more day and we'll be out of here and I don't care what happens to them women.

It was eleven o'clock and Suzanne, the speech therapist, had arrived for Paul's session.

"He won't be long. He should be back any minute. May I get you some coffee while you wait?" Rebecca asked.

"No thank you, Mrs. Devon. I'm fine. I've had enough coffee already this morning," Suzanne said.

It was eleven forty-five and Paul still had not come back. Rebecca was becoming concerned. As she looked out of the kitchen window toward the cemetery, she thought she heard a whimper. She walked over and opened the door.

"Oh dear God!" she screamed. "Beau, what has happened to you? Where's Paul?"

Suzanne heard her scream and ran out to the kitchen.

Beau had come inside and was lying on the floor near the door.

Blood was all over his fur and face and there was a large gash on his head.

Rebecca grabbed a kitchen towel and wet it. She tried to get the blood off of him, but he growled at her. He had never done that before to anyone.

"I think I better go look for Paul. I have a feeling that something terrible has happened to him. Beau never leaves Paul when they go out for a walk," Rebecca said.

"I'll come with you, Mrs. Devon," Suzanne said.

The two women were almost running as they headed toward the family cemetery.

"Paul! Paul!" Rebecca screamed.

When they reached the mausoleum, they saw a pool of blood on the marble walkway.

"I know he's dead! I just know it!" Rebecca cried out for Paul, but to no avail.

"Mrs. Devon, look on the iron grill," Suzanne said.

Rebecca ran up to the door and grabbed the folded piece of paper.

"They've kidnapped Paul," she said.

Suzanne took the paper out of Rebecca's hand and read it. "Oh, no, they have the two women too!" she exclaimed.

Both women ran back to the house as fast as they could. Rebecca dialed the police and told them what had happened. She was hysterical.

"Hang on, someone will be right over," the voice said.

Rebecca reached in a kitchen drawer and found Jason Rowe's number. She said, "Suzanne, will you please call this number and get Jason?"

The young woman dialed the number and Mary Ellen Weatherstone answered.

"I need to talk to Jason Rowe, right now. It's urgent," Suzanne said.

When he got on the line, Suzanne explained who she was and why she was calling.

"I'll be right there," he said, and ran out of the front door.

6

"There are police cars everywhere! I wonder what's going on?" Charles said to Ben as they drove past the post office/country store.

As they headed toward West Knob, they could hear sirens everywhere. When they turned up the long driveway to the mansion, they saw two police cars and Jason Rowe's car parked out front. Ben pulled up in front of the house, where they both jumped out and ran inside. When Rebecca saw Charles, she ran over and began sobbing in his arms. Suzanne explained what had happened during the morning. Charles turned pale as he listened to what had happened. Police were all over the grounds, searching in every direction. Jason went outside with one of the officers and headed to the family cemetery. Ben went to the kitchen and found Beau still stretched out near the door. Even with all of the commotion, he hadn't moved. He then went out to the truck, got a blanket and without a struggle, he wrapped him up and headed out through the living room to the truck.

"I'll be right back. I'm taking Beau down to the Vet. Suzanne, will you call him and tell him I'm on my way?" Ben asked.

Suzanne phoned the animal doctor and explained the situation. The Vet was only two miles down the road from West Knob so it wouldn't take Ben long to get back.

Rebecca was almost inconsolable and Charles was just about paralyzed with fear for his son.

Suzanne went in to the kitchen and made a cup of tea for Rebecca. One officer was questioning Charles. Suzanne handed the cup to Mrs. Devon and sat down next to her trying to console her. Another officer came over and started questioning the two women. Suzanne explained again everything that had happened that morning. He had the ransom note in his hand and when he was finished questioning the women, he walked over and showed it to Charles.

A little while later, Ben walked in to the living room and went over to Charles. The officer filled Ben in on what had happened.

"Charles, come with me," Ben said. "I'm going out to the cemetery."

The two men went out the back door and headed to the family-resting place. When they got there, Jason was looking around the mausoleum. The pool of blood was still on the marble walkway and a bloody rock lay nearby. One of the officers was dusting the door for fingerprints. Another officer was coming out of the woods with a search dog. As he went passed the mausoleum, the dog stopped and sniffed the blood and rock then continued north out through the hemlocks.

"This is unbelievable! They not only have Paul, but they have the women too," Charles exclaimed.

Pulling out his cell phone, Jason said, "I'm going to call the McCartys. I want them to be prepared for whatever happens." He walked a few feet away and dialed their number.

"Hello, Sarah, this is Jason Rowe," he said. "I have some news for you."

He explained everything that had happened and told her the police would probably be there shortly. He asked her to get a hold of the Vermillions and he would get back with them soon.

The police were putting up yellow crime scene tape all around the mausoleum and the wooded areas behind the cemetery. The search dog kept coming back to the pool of blood and the tomb of Joseph.

Sirens could be heard all over the valley. All afternoon the police were out and about West Knob combing the two hundred and fifty acres.

"Jason, I don't know what to do about the ransom money. I called my bank in Philadelphia and told them to get the money ready and have a courier bring it up here. I want to see Paul and the women before

I turn over the money. I'd give everything I have to get them back, but there's no guarantee that they are still alive," Charles said.

"Hang on Charles. We have two days. Captain Moore, from the State Police, is on his way over here now and we'll talk to him then. He probably has a plan and right now all we can do is wait," Jason said.

The frantic search continued into the evening. The police put up search lights out at the cemetery and into the surrounding woods. Now two dogs were searching the grounds but they always came back to the cemetery.

It was dark now. Two police officers stayed at the house in case the Devons received any phone calls from the kidnappers as one officer stood guard at the cemetery. Mrs. Devon asked Suzanne if she would stay overnight and she had agreed. It was the housekeeper's day off, but when she heard about what had happened, she came over to the house and prepared sandwiches and some light food. It was going to be a long night and the next couple of days would be exhausting.

Ben, Charles and Jason sat at the kitchen table going over the horrible events of the day and discussed who could be responsible for the kidnappings.

Jason asked Ben, "How is Beau doing?"

"The Vet called a little while ago. He said Beau would be all right. He stitched his head and gave him something for the pain. He's going to keep him a day or two just to make sure," he said.

"I was out looking around the cemetery again and the search dogs kept coming back to the same spot. I didn't see anything except the pool of blood, which the police figured, was from Beau. They took samples just to be sure in case it belonged to someone else besides the dog. Everything looked in place...just a crack in the marble walkway and a few scratches on the iron slab in the back of the mausoleum," Jason told him.

"What do you mean cracked marble?" Ben asked. "I was their yesterday and the walkway was fine. I polished the door and walked all around and I didn't see any scratches on the slab."

"Charles is there anyway that anyone could get into the

mausoleum? I know that it is a long shot, but could it be possible?" Jason asked.

No, not at all! Only Ben and I have a key. No one has been in there since Joseph was laid to rest. That's just insane! What possible reason would anyone have to get inside? Joseph is dead. Why would they want him? It just doesn't make any sense," Charles said.

"How about the steel slab on the back?" Jason asked.

"I don't think so," Charles said. "It's bolted with heavy steel bolts. We were waiting for the stained-glass window to arrive and replaced it. No one could get in there without taking the panel off and that would be almost impossible."

It was apparent that Charles was getting upset over all of the questioning.

"How about the scratches on the panel? How would they have gotten there?" Jason persisted.

The three men just looked at each other and seemed to be thinking the same thing at the same time.

"Charles, get the key and a flashlight. We have to take another look out there," Jason said.

All three men went running out through the woods to the cemetery.

"Where are you going ?" the officer on guard asked.

"We're going to open the mausoleum. My son Joseph may have been taken," Charles said.

"I'm gong to have to call Captain Moore first," he said.

"We don't have time!" Charles yelled, as he pushed the yellow crime scene tape aside.

His hand was shaking so badly he could hardly get the key in the lock. Finally, the iron gate gave way and then the wooden door. Ben shined the light inside fearing what they would see.

The tomb was musty from being closed for so long and the light made eerie shadows against the wall.

"Oh, my God! Shine the light to the right again. It looks like there's something back in the corner," Jason said.

Charles was still shaking as he moved closer to the figure in the corner. Even in the semi-darkness, they could see that it was Paul.

"Paul, Paul!" Charles yelled. "Is he dead? Is he dead?"

Jason leaned over to check the motionless body.

"No, he is still breathing," Jason said, and pulled the tape off of his mouth.

The three men carried Paul outside and laid him on the walkway. Charles held him close as Ben cut the tape off of his arms and legs. The officer went inside the tomb, looked around and locked the door behind him.

Out in the air and without the tape on his mouth, Paul began to breathe a little better.

"My God, my God! You're alive," Charles cried out, as tears filled his eyes.

Charles, Ben, Jason and the officer carried Paul back to the mansion.

"Call the doctor," Charles shouted, as they entered the backdoor.

When Rebecca saw him, she broke down in tears. The two officers in the house couldn't believe what they were seeing. Everyone had thought the worst. They laid Paul on the sofa and covered him with a blanket. Slowly, he was starting to come around.

"I'll call Captain Moore," the officer said.

"Wait. We have Paul, but whoever did this still has the women. We can't let them know we found him. Tell Captain Moore the situation and ask him to come over here right now," Jason said.

He's right," Charles said. We have to keep this quiet until we get the women. If they find out we have Paul, you don't know what they might do to the women. I believe whoever did this can't be far away and they must have been familiar with West Knob. A whole list of the men, who had built the mausoleum, flashed through his mind. He couldn't single out any one of them who could have been responsible for this.

For Paul's sake, it was a good thing that he was unconscious. The horror of what happened would have been too much to bear. To Charles and Rebecca, seeing Paul was like seeing a ghost. They were both thinking the worst and they never expected to see him alive again. Neither could believe what they had done to him… and to Joseph.

Now they had to get the women.

When Captain Moore arrived back at West Knob, he informed every one of his plans. "I've ordered my officers to start searching tonight. We can't wait until morning. I have men in every part of Mercyville. Their orders are to search everything...houses, cabins, trailers and barns...any place they could hide someone. No one will be exempt. I have two more teams of search dogs fanning out down along the creek. We have to find those women now and if they are still alive, it will be a miracle," he said.

The police were at the McCartys' house shortly after the disappearance of Paul Devon. They had informed both the families of the contents of the ransom note. Neither family was wealthy, but both had secured and pooled their resources for the safe return of the women.

Three families of Mercyville had been emotionally torn apart and now at least two had some hope for their loved ones. The third family had come back from the depth of despair to the elation of having their cherished son returned. Only the Devons could truly understand the agony of the McCartys and the Vermillions.

The phone rang at West Knob. Charles picked it up not knowing if it would be the kidnappers at the other end.

"Hello, Mr. Devon. This is Allan McCarty. We are sorry about your son. The police told us about the ransom note this afternoon. We don't have a lot of money, but we would like you to have what we have toward the ransom. I can have one of the officers bring it over to West Knob. Again, we are truly sorry about your son," the man said.

"Allan," Charles said. "Don't concern yourself about the money. I have it all taken care of. At this point, all I want is the safe return of everyone involved. No amount of money can replace those we love and if my family can help you in any way, please call. We'll be here at Wes Knob. Thank you, Allan, for calling."

West Knob was settling into a quieter mode than the afternoon. The doctor had come right after Paul was found. He reported that Paul was on good health and the only thing he needed was a good night's rest. Rebecca and Suzanne sat in the quiet living room trying to digest the nightmare of the day. The housekeeper had filled the refrigerator with ready to eat food before she went home. Jason had left to go over to the McCartys' house. Charles was talking to the two police officers that were staying for the night. Ben returned to his apartment for a few hours of sleep; if that was possible.

The Devons were prepared to pay the ransom for the women against the wishes of Captain Moore. He wanted to know for sure that the women were still alive before any ransom was paid.

Everyone was mentally fatigued. Just thinking about what kind of a person could do what they did to Paul was sickening and to desecrate Joseph's tomb was beyond despicable.

In less than twenty-eight hours the families would know if the women were alive. All they could do now was hope and pray.

7

In the darkened loft, Mary McCarty and Leslie Vermillion could see the lights coming from the road to Edwardton flashing on the walls of their cell of hell. All afternoon, they had heard the sirens of police cars and they wondered what was happening. Both hoped they were coming for them…coming to get them out of their midnight-blue hall of terror.

Rich Aaron was out on the porch of the cabin watching the flashing lights of the police cars. All afternoon they heard the sirens coming and going. All afternoon he thought about the sunny beaches of Florida and getting out of Mercyville.

His thought was broken as he saw lights coming through the hemlock forest in front of him. Out to the left, a half-mile away, he saw a police car with its flashing lights pull up to a cabin.

"Get out here, Tom! Hurry up!" Rich said.

Tom went out on the porch to see what was wrong.

"I think they're searching all of the houses! What are we going to do? It looks like they are searching everything. What if they come in here? Now what, huh, now what?" Rich said, in total panic.

"Just shut up! Let me think a minute! We're not having the whole damn thing ruined now. In a little over twenty-eight hours, we'll be out of here. Get inside! Take that tape, go upstairs and tape them women's mouth shut! We don't need them screaming if they do come here. Hurry up!" Tom commanded.

The door to the loft opened and the light from downstairs flooded up into the second floor. Rich was a silhouette against the light as he moved toward Mary's bed.

"What are you doing?" she asked.

"I'm going to shut you two up." He tore a long strip of tape to use on the women. Mary struggled to turn away from him. He put his knee on her chest to hold her still while he taped her mouth. When he was finished with her, he went over to Leslie. As he leaned over her, she kicked him in the stomach. It infuriated him and he felt like slapping her.

"You are lucky that you are still alive," he said. "I should kill you right now. No, I should have killed you weeks ago. Tom was right. Getting rid of you two would have been a lot easier. He sat on her as he taped her mouth shut. When he was finished, he left and went back downstairs and again the room was pitch black. Now that they couldn't even talk to each other, they were more alone than ever.

"What if they come in here to search the place? Then what?" Rich yelled to Tom.

"Damn it, Rich, just shut up!" Tom said. "Get over there and we'll move the bookcase in front of the door to the loft."

"It's too heavy to move with all of that stuff on it," Rich moaned.

"If you ever want to see a sandy beach, you'll move it damn fast!" Tom yelled.

It took all the strength the two men had but slowly they moved the bookcase into place, concealing the door to the loft.

"There!" Tom said. "No one will suspect that there's a door behind that case. Straighten up the rug and pull that chair over here. Now, get a hold of yourself. It's almost over."

They had just finished with the bookcase when a police car, with flashing lights, pulled up outside of the cabin.

"Oh, my God! Now what are we going to do?" Rich cried.

"Shut up! Pull yourself together. I'll do the talking," Tom said.

Just then, there was a knock at the cabin door. Tom opened the door and was greeted by two Highway Patrolmen.

"We're here in regard to the disappearance of Paul Devon and the two missing women from Mercyville. We are searching all of the buildings in the area," the officer said.

"Come in. We heard about the missing women, but we didn't know anything about the Devon man," Tom said.

"Do you mind if we look around?" the officer asked.

"No, go right ahead," Tom said.

Rich Aaron's heart was pounding. His palms had become sweaty and his mouth was so dry, he could hardly speak. He was about to go into a full-fledged panic attack as the officer's eyes flashed back and forth over the bookcase. He walked over to the bookcase and closely examined some of the items on the shelves. Then the officer searching the cabin came back into the room and spoke.

"Everything looks fine here. Thank you for your cooperation. If you should hear or see anything out of the ordinary, please give us a call," he said.

Tom thanked the two officers as they left. Rich collapsed on the chair next to the bookcase as his heart continued to beat out of control.

The Aarons had passed the unexpected intrusion.

"I'm taking the truck to Edwardton to gas-up and put a call in to our neighbors, the Devons. They better have the money or nobody will live. By now that Devon kid is probably dead anyway," Tom said.

"Well, what should I do if the police come back?" Rich whined.

"Well, Rich, why don't you just invite them in for a beer!" Tom said, angrily. "You'd better straighten yourself out! You're so damn nervous, you're driving me crazy! You can't come unglued now! They were here once! Do you really think that they're going to bother to come back again? Think, Rich! Just start thinking and quit your whining.

"Three days from now, we'll be in the Sunshine State and nobody will ever know, as they say 'Who dunnit!' While this town is still trying to figure out what hit 'em, we'll be checking out the beach babes in bikinis. I'll be back in a little while. Just try to relax, will you?"

Patrol cars were going in every direction around Mercyville. No household was off limits no matter who they were. The country store/post office was searched again along with the adjacent lumber mill. Even the Mercyville Church was not overlooked and was thoroughly examined inside and out.

Officers were stopping at every building along Branch Creek Road.

Alison and Matt Wallace were sitting on their deck watching the commotion in the valley when a State Trooper pulled into their driveway. Matt went down the stairs to meet them.

"We're searching every house in the area for the missing Devon man and the two Mercyville women. Do you mind if we have a look around?" the officer asked.

"No, not at all. You can go in here through the studio and upstairs or follow me up the deck," Matt said.

One trooper went in the downstairs and the other one followed Matt up to the deck.

"Alison and I will wait out here," Matt said. "Help yourself."

In a few minutes, both of the troopers came out on the deck.

"Thank you for your cooperation. If anything out of the norm occurs, give us a call."

After they left, Alison said, "This whole situation is frightening. I was never afraid of being out here alone, but now I'm really on edge. I hope they'll find them soon. Their families must be going crazy with worry."

"This is the last place I would have expected something like this to happen. I don't think you should go out painting any more until these disappearances are solved. I'd rather you stay close to home. It would make me feel a lot more at ease," Matt said.

All night long, police lights flashed through the mountains and in the valley. Family after family was eliminated from any possible connection to the disappearances.

The police pulled up in front of Martin Benson's fence. To their surprise, he was outside with a kerosene lantern putting up more signs along his fence line. Evidently, the Edwardton Hardware store had a fifty-percent off sale on signs, which Martin couldn't resist. Now, along with the multitude of already weathering signs, several new renditions, in fancy script, declared, "Private Drive", "No Exit", "No

Solicitors" and "Dead End".

"Good evening," the officer said. "We're searching every property in regard to the disappearance of the missing Mercyville women and Paul Devon. Do you mind if we look around your place?"

"I don't know nothing about them women and I didn't know that the Devon kid was missing," Martin growled.

"Well, sir, do you mind if we look around?" the officer asked.

As he held the lantern a little higher to get a better look at the officer's face, Martin said, "Can't you people read these signs? I don't like strangers snooping around my place."

"Sir, if you don't let us search, we'll have to get a search warrant," the officer said. "We're not accusing you of any involvement. We're searching everybody's property in and around Mercyville."

Martin thought for a moment, then said, "Go ahead. Look around, but make it quick. I'm busy!"

The officers walked down the driveway marked "Private" and went in to the cabin. By looking at the outside of the property, they were surprised when they went inside. The cabin was small, but everything inside was immaculate. The single bed, next to the wood stove, was made and at the foot of it, blankets were neatly folded. A table and two chairs were placed near the kitchen area. Several shelves held canned goods, pots and dishes. A small open-shelf cabinet held cereals, coffee and other dry products. A huge braided rug covered a large portion of the pine-planked floor. In one corner of the cabin was an open wardrobe with neatly hung clothes. To look at Martin, you would have never expected he had such organizational skills.

The officers walked out of the cabin to where he was standing.

"Are there any other buildings on your property, sir?" an officer asked.

"Yeah, over that hill I have a springhouse. There ain't anything in there either," Martin said.

"Well, we'll just take a quick look," the officer said.

Martin led the way through the trees with the kerosene lantern.

"There it is," he said, pointing to the structure.

The officers opened the wood plank door and went inside. Standing in the water, that passed through the small stone building, were two large milk cans with butcher-paper wrapped meat. Only a small table, used for cutting fish and meat, stood in the corner. Like his cabin, the springhouse was almost surgically clean.

They walked out of the springhouse, and thanked Martin before they headed back out the driveway.

Martin was alone again behind his world of signs.

After the officers left, Martin resumed the nighttime decorating of his fence. He put up the last sign and was walking back toward his cabin when all of a sudden; he heard a vehicle screeching and then a loud crash.

Someone had done the unthinkable! They had collided with Martin's perimeter of signs, taking out a large section of newly posted directives.

He heard a vehicle revving its engine and he was sure he had heard the same thing before. As it flew past his driveway, he could see that it was a pickup truck, just like the one he used to own. He was so infuriated at the demise of part of his fence that he jumped in his truck and gave chase.

Both the pickup and Martin were barely navigating the winding mountain road. Four miles later the pickup turned into a narrow dirt driveway. Martin pulled his truck up on the edge of the hard road. He got out and quietly moved through the woods up to the cabin where the old truck was parked. He was ready to kill the person who had destroyed his fence. As he walked past an open cabin window he heard two men screaming at each other. He stood frozen in the dark and listened to the ensuing argument.

"What the hell were you thinking, Rich? Why did you bring them women downstairs? What happened to the bookcase? It looks like a damn bomb went off in here! You've lost it this time!" Tom yelled.

"Hold on Tom! It wasn't my fault —," Rich started to explain.

"What the hell do you mean it wasn't your fault? You're the only one here besides them damn women, you idiot!" Tom bellowed.

"Ok, ok! Here's what happened," Rich said. "Just after you left,

I heard a crash upstairs, but I couldn't go up because the bookcase was in the way and I couldn't move it. So, I started throwing the stuff off of it. I guess it got a little out of hand. Anyway, I finally got upstairs. That McCarty woman must have knocked the flashlight that I left up there off of the table. I just forgot to bring it downstairs last night. So I thought I'd get 'em down here where I could watch 'em. I handcuffed one in each bedroom. It's ok, Tom, it's ok!"

"Get this mess cleaned up! I've had enough damn problems tonight," Tom said. "I called the Devons. I warned them they better have the money or the kid and the women are dead. I told'em not to try to follow us. He said he had the money and it would be there. He would take it to the church himself and he wanted proof that they are all still alive… so I hung up.

"On the way back from Edwardton, a deer ran out in front of the truck. I swerved to miss it and plowed into that Benson guy's fence. He started chasing me down the mountain but I got away from him. It's one damn catastrophe around here after another! I'll be glad when it's all over and we're out of here."

Martin was standing in the dark in total shock from what he had heard. A million thoughts raced through his mind at the same time. "I've got to get out of here! Maybe I should just go to the police. No, I'll go to the Devons' place. Maybe these men have the Devon kid here too. I've got to get out of here and fast!" he thought.

Slowly and quietly, Martin made his way back to his truck. He was afraid to start the engine for fear it would be heard so he released the brake and drifted down the road toward the Devon estate. When he felt it was safe, he started the engine and headed for West Knob.

When Martin reached the estate, the front gate was open. Slowly, he drove up the long driveway. He parked this truck behind the police car and walked up to the front door and knocked. When a police officer answered the door, Martin asked to see Mr. Devon. Just then, Charles came to the door. He remembered Martin and not in a pleasurable way.

"Let him in," Charles told the officer.

Martin followed him into the living room.

"What is it that you want?" asked Charles.

Martin explained everything. From the demise of his fence, the mountain chase, the two men in the cabin and what they said about the women.

"Martin, have a seat," Charles said.

One of the officers called Captain Moore and relayed the latest twist in the kidnapping saga.

When the officer hung up, he told Martin to stay there until the Captain arrived.

Rebecca had just come downstairs from checking on Paul and was informed of what Martin had said.

"This has been an unbelievable day. What else could possibly happen?" Rebecca wondered.

She walked over to where Martin was sitting.

"Martin, I'm Rebecca Devon," she said. "I don't believe we've ever met. May I get you a cup of coffee?"

Martin accepted her invitation. Actually, the way he felt now, he could have had something a little stronger than coffee. He seldom drank any alcoholic beverages but he felt this was a time of deep need and he was considering it for medicinal purposes.

Ben Jenkins had a few hours of sleep and had come back to the house. If there was nothing immediate that he could do, at least he was there for moral support.

Charles informed Ben of the latest developments regarding the missing women.

The quiet evening of sitting in the living room was now turning into a repeat of the afternoon. Only tonight, their prayers and hopes seemed to be closer to being answered.

8

For the third time in the last twelve hours, Captain Moore returned to West Knob. He had worked on many cases during his long career but beyond a shadow of a doubt, this was the most bizarre.

When he entered the mansion, he went straight to Martin and asked him to explain everything that had happened.

Again, Martin reported, in detail, all that had occurred in the last hours. The more he recounted the events, the more he realized how involved he was becoming in the return of the captives.

When Martin had finished talking to the Captain, the Captain said, "Martin, there is one more thing you should know."

At this point, Martin felt like he didn't need anymore surprises. He believed he was in this thing deep enough and sinking deeper with every passing minute.

"Paul Devon is alive. He is upstairs resting," he said.

Martin's eyes became wide with a look of surprise and he didn't think he was hearing right.

"How can that be?" Martin asked.

Charles explained everything that had happened during the day.

Martin was visibly shaken when he heard about the opening of the mausoleum. "How could anyone do that?"

The Captain contacted the officers who had searched the Aarons' cabin. He needed to know the layout of the building and just where the women were located.

Shortly after the call, the two officers arrived.

The officer who searched the cabin made a sketch of the floor plan. Now the Captain needed a plan to get the women without putting them in any further danger. What he needed was the distraction of both men and he needed to get them outside of the cabin and away from the women.

What he needed was Martin's help.

After the Captain informed those who would be involved in the recovery as to what he wanted them to do, he directed his next thought to Martin.

"Martin, I need you to get both men outside of the cabin. I need you to cause a diversion outside so our officers can get inside. Are you willing to do that?" he asked.

Martin was dumbfounded. He wondered how he got his self involved in all of this. How would he get them outside? For the first time Martin wasn't agitated, he was damn scared!

"Here's what we'll do," Captain Moore said, as everyone moved in close to be sure they wouldn't miss a detail. He proceeded to explain the plan of recovery. "We'll leave in a half-hour."

Martin just sat there staring at his feet. "Why did they have to hit my fence?" he thought. "If it weren't for them Aarons', I would be home sound asleep in bed."

"Mrs. Devon do you think I could have another cup of coffee?" he asked.

It was two o'clock in the morning and the Aaron brothers were asleep for the last time in their cabin. Soon they would be out of Mercyville for good. Soon it would all be over and they would be rich forever.

Eight of Moore's men and Martin drove to the Aarons' cabin. They parked their vehicles a good distance away from the cabin as not to be heard. The officers crept through the hemlocks and toward the cabin as Martin sat in his truck at the end of the Aarons' driveway. As they neared the cabin, they divided up and surrounded the perimeters of the building. Two officers would stand, on either side of the door. As the men came out of the cabin, they would apprehend them. The night was eerily still except for the howl of a distant coyote.

When the men were all set to secure the cabin, the Captain gave Martin the signal to go.

Martin turned on the lights of his truck, revved up the engine and sped down the dirt driveway. When he got near the old-parked truck, he stopped, kept revving up this engine and blowing his horn.

Inside of the cabin, both of the sleeping brothers were startled into a semi-state of consciousness.

"What the hell is that?" Tom screamed, as he jumped out of bed and headed for the front door with Rich close at his heels.

He flew open the door of the cabin and stepped out on to the darkened porch to find out what was going on. Still groggy from sleep, they didn't expect to be grabbed from behind. With very little struggle both men were wrestled to the floor of the porch. Two officers ran inside and in moments, the captive women were finally free and both broke down in tears.

Immediately after the capture, Captain Moore phoned the McCartys' home with the news.

Martin, a non-complex man, sat in his truck overwhelmed by the course of the events in the last few hours.

The officers put the women in the patrol car and headed for the McCartys' house as the Aaron brothers headed for jail.

In the middle of the night, lights went on throughout Mercyville as word spread of the recovery of the women.

Before he left, the Captain went over to the truck and thanked Martin for all of his help.

As Martin drove home, he was still shaking from the whole experience. (or maybe that second cup of coffee) All he wanted to do was get behind the protection of his fence and go to sleep. Maybe, he thought, when he woke up, it would all have been a bad dream.

The Vermillions and Jason were at the McCartys' house when the police arrived with the two women. The reunion was absolutely joyous. Neither family could fathom the elation of holding them in their arms. It seemed, they had come back from the dead. Weeks of anguish rushed out in a flood of tears. It was over. The nightmare was finally over.

It was eleven o'clock in the morning when Captain Moore arrived at the McCartys' house to talk to Mary and Leslie. The women had slept very little with the excitement of being home.

"I would like to know how it came about that you were kidnapped?" he asked.

Mary spoke first. "I was on my way to Edwardton. As I came around the bend in the road, there was a man lying face down in the road. I thought that maybe he was dead because he wasn't moving so I stopped and got out. When I got up close to him, I could see he was wearing a mask. In the same instant another man in a ski mask grabbed me from behind and they forced me into their truck. Then they brought me to their cabin and that is where I had been the entire time. I have never seen their faces."

"The same thing happened to me," Leslie said. "I couldn't imagine what could have happened to the person in the road. Looking back, I should have been more cautious but I thought I could help. When they brought me back to the cabin is when I learned that Mary was here too. They kept us handcuffed to the beds the whole time. The only time they let us up was to use the bathroom. Two nights ago, the one called Rich, left his flashlight on the table next to Mary's bed. She was able to reach it and kept blinking it on and off by the window hoping that someone would see it. Tonight she tried to reach the flashlight again but she knocked it over and it fell on the floor. Rich went running up the steps, grabbed Mary and took her downstairs and then he came up and got me. After that I didn't see Mary again until the police came.

"Thank you, ladies. I know you're exhausted, so get some rest. Everyone is elated that both of you survived the ordeal. I will want to talk to both of you later on," the Captain said, as he got up to leave.

Two days later, sanity was beginning to settle back into West Knob. Paul had recovered but did not remember what had happened. The last thing he remembered was a masked man grabbing him. The next thing he recalled was waking up in the living room. No one was going to tell him, at least not right now, what had really taken place and where he was found. There would be time for that later.

As Charles got up from the breakfast table, he told the family that he had some business to take care of in Mercyville and would be back shortly. With that said, he left and headed toward the road to Edwardton.

A few miles outside of Mercyville, he pulled up to the fence where Martin was chopping wood. He was back into his regular routine.

Charles walked over to the closed gate and called to Martin that he would like to talk to him.

Reluctantly, Martin walked up to the gate.

"Martin, I want to thank you for all you contributed in getting the women back. It really was a courageous thing that you did. To show my appreciation, I would like you to consider if you would like to hunt at West Knob?" Charles said, with a smile on his face. "That would be just during hunting season only."

Martin didn't expect that at all. He was rather embarrassed, in respect to his last hunting activities involving Charles Devon and West Knob.

"Well, ah, ah, yeah," Martin stammered. "I would like to do that. Thank you."

"By the way, I'd like you to accept this check. If it weren't for you, I don't know what the outcome would have been for the women," Charles said.

Martin looked at the check and tears filled his eyes. No one had ever given him anything, let alone a check for ten thousand dollars.

Humbly, Martin thanked Mr. Devon.

"We'll see you later Martin," Charles said, and got in his car and headed back to West Knob.

Martin had something that he wanted to do in Mercyville and now was the best time to get it done.

There was a knock on the door of the McCartys' house. Sarah McCarty answered it. When she opened the door, a neatly dressed man in coveralls introduced himself as Martin Benson. He reached in the pocket of his shirt and handed her a gold bracelet with a robin on it.

"I think Mary lost this," Martin said. Then he turned and walked away.

All was well once again in Mercyville.

The Devons, McCartys and Vermillions were united with their loved ones.

The conclave of opinion makers, at the country store/ post office, were once again in good spirits at the large, round table with the always on coffeepot.

Alison Wallace was able to go out painting again.

Beau, the canine of West Knob, had recovered from the injury to his head and was back chasing squirrels and rabbits.

The bear at the recreation ground had been relocated in an undisclosed area one hundred miles north of Mercyville and the Dumpster was no longer tapped each night.

The prayers of those at the Mercyville church, for the kidnapped victims, had been answered.

Signs advertising "Free Stuff" were once again scattered occasionally on a few lawns throughout the valley.

It seemed that Mercyville was back to normal with the exception of one thing.

Martin Benson's perimeter line of fence no longer had warning signs on it. He had taken them all down except for one on the front gate. It was a large white sign with red letters. It read, "Welcome".

9

Two years had passed and nothing out of norm had happened in the 'Plain Jane' village of Mercyville. All of its citizenry were back to their regular routines. The tourist and hunting seasons had been good to the community. Rarely did the topic of the kidnapped women and Paul Devon come up any more. It was in the past and the people of the village didn't live in the past. With the long winter behind them, summer activities were on the rise and outdoor socializing had begun once again. Mercyville was truly a Garden of Eden in the Endless Mountains.

The country store was busy supplying campers with their outdoor needs. Martin Benson had stacked firewood by his gate with the Welcome sign and was having trouble keeping up with the demand from the flood of city folks turned campers. At the recreation ground, Frank Townsend and his wife had gotten a new, bear-proof second home on wheels and were happily settled by a stream, under a spreading oak tree.

It was almost noon when a young woman came in to the country store. She walked over to the cashier and asked for directions to the Devon estate. The lady behind the counter drew a small map to the mansion. The cashier knew she wasn't a local, as everyone around Mercyville knew where the mansion was located. The young woman thanked the cashier and left the store.

Shortly, the doorbell rang at West Knob. As Charles opened the door, he saw a beautiful young woman with two handsome little boys.

"Mr. Devon, I'm Paula O'Brien. May I come in? I would like to speak to you," she said.

Charles showed her the way to the living room where Mrs. Devon was writing letters. She stopped when the young woman entered the room. Charles introduced Paula to Rebecca.

As the young lady started to speak, Rebecca couldn't take her eyes off of the two handsome children.

"I know this is going to be a shock to both of you, but Joseph and I were engaged. The night that he was killed, he way on his way home to tell you that we were getting married. I was to come home with him but I was a medical student at the time and at the last minute I was called to work in the emergency room. I was devastated when I found out that Joseph had been killed. I was a month pregnant with his child, or as I later found out children.

"Looking back, I know we should have waited until I was out of school. I felt that my whole world had collapsed and I just wanted to die. It wasn't until the boys were born that I was able to take back control of my life. My parents helped me with the children while I finished my internship. If it were not for them, I don't know what I would have done. Mr. and Mrs. Devon, these are your grandson's, Charles and Joseph."

Rebecca was in a state of shock. Not only were the memories of Joseph flooding back in to her mind but also the thought of grandchildren overwhelmed her.

" Indeed this is quite a surprise and a shock! I couldn't help but see the resemblance between the children and Joseph when he was that age. I thought it was my imagination. Forgive me for being so surprised. The thought of grandchildren never occurred to me after Joseph's death," she said.

"What are your plans for you and the boys?" Charles asked, almost at a loss for words.

"I apologize again for the shock both of you must feel. I guess I should have come here sooner," Paula said.

"I just set up my medical practice in Philadelphia. I wanted to be close to my family, especially while the boys are young. They were to the point where they were starting to ask about their father. I felt it was time to let them know that they had another family besides my own. When they are old enough to understand, I will tell them what happened to Joseph.

"I don't want to take up any more of your time. I have to get back to Philadelphia. One more thing, I knew about Paul and his accident. I have often wondered how he was doing?"

"Paul had a complete recovery. It was a long, hard struggle for him but he is fine now. He and his speech therapist, Suzanne, were married a year ago," Mrs. Devon said.

Just then Ben and Paul came in from their walk.

"Ben, Paul, I'd like you to meet Paula O'Brien and Paul, I would like you to meet your nephews, Charles and Joseph," Rebecca said with a smile.

Paul's mouth just dropped open but he was too stunned to speak.

Realizing his shock, Rebecca said, "Don't worry, Paul, I'll explain it all to you later."

"I really must leave now. I'll leave my address and phone number. I hope, when you are in Philadelphia, you will come to see the boys," Paula said, as she walked toward the front door with the boys.

"Paula, would you mind if I kissed my grandsons good-bye?" Rebecca asked.

"I think they would like that," she replied.

As the Devons watched them leave, Charles turned to his wife and said, "I knew that I bought that carousel horse for a reason!"

He realized that the Charles Devon line had continued after all.

Rebecca said, "Needless to say, Charles; this is a surprise and a shock. I guess all we can expect out of life, is to expect the unexpected."

10

As the card with number eleven flashed up again, the hammer slammed down for the last time. Sold for ninety-eight thousand dollars to the man in the blue shirt.

A tall man, with black hair, walked up to the podium, took out his checkbook, and made the sale final.

After just over two years, closure had finally come to the era of the Aarons. Their cabin had set empty and the grounds had become over grown. After what had happened there, none of the locals were the least bit interested in acquiring the property. By the time the Aaron brothers got out of jail, their accommodations would probably be more like a nursing home; if they were lucky enough to last that long.

The new owner of the Aarons' property was Franz Kohler, an art dealer from New York City. Evidently, the kidnapping that had happened there was unknown to him or if it was, it didn't matter.

He had asked Jerry Zimmerman, the auctioneer, if he knew of anyone who would be interested in cleaning up the property and working as a part-time caretaker? Jerry volunteered his services every year at the Volunteer Fire Department Auction and he knew a number of the locals. He recommended Martin Benson and thought he would be a dependable worker. It just happened that Martin was at the auction hoping to buy a few tools.

The auctioneer spotted Martin in the crowd and waved him to come over. When he reached the auctioneer, Jerry introduced him to the new property owner, Franz Kohler.

"I was wondering if you would be interested in cleaning up this property and possibly working as a part-time caretaker?" Franz asked.

Martin didn't know what to say. This was the first time he had been near the property since the night he helped apprehend the Aaron brothers. Even the thought of that night sent shivers down his spine and being there today brought back all of the memories of the kidnappings.

"If it's money, Martin, you can be assured you'll be well paid for your labor," Franz said.

"No, it's not the money. I was just remembering what had happened here two ago," Martin replied.

"Yes, I'm aware of the kidnappings but it really doesn't make any difference to me. I plan on putting up another house and keeping the cabin as a guesthouse. So, I hope you'll consider the employment offer," he said.

"Well, yes...I'll do the work for you. If you want me to, I can start tomorrow," Martin said.

"Good. I'll be here at nine o'clock and we can go over what I want done," Franz said.

As Martin loaded his newly acquired tools in the back of the truck, the auction crowd started breaking up.

Driving back home, Martin thought about the Aarons' cabin and everything that had happened there. He was glad for the work, but he wasn't sure it was the right place for him. He remembered Tom Aaron tearing out his fence line and now he would be part-time caretaker for the Aarons' place. The whole thing seemed rather ironic to him and he just hoped he was making the right move. As he drove up to his gate with the large red *welcome* sign, there were two campers waiting to buy firewood. The number of campers had doubled and it kept him busy cutting wood. Ever since he took down his array of warning signs, people seemed to him to be more friendly. Of course it didn't occur to him that it could have been the other way around.

The last two years had been good to Martin. With the money Charles Devon gave him for helping recover the kidnapped women, he opened his first ever savings account at the Edwardton bank. Now that he had a little money in his pocket, his diet of venison and trout was supplemented occasionally with beef and chicken. Even his wardrobe had been expanded to a few new sets of coveralls and shirts. "Life is good," he thought. There wasn't much more that he needed except for one thing. He wanted a dog. It had been a long time since Red, his mixed bloodhound, died. It seemed as though he feared getting another dog because losing it became to hard. Red was his close companion; well, maybe his only companion. But time had passed and he was willing to take another chance and find a dog. Martin had learned in the past two years to reach out and take chances. His world had started to expand beyond the perimeters of his fence and he was enjoying it.

Franz Kohler was standing on the porch of the cabin at nine o'clock when Martin Benson pulled up and got out of his truck. Evidently, he had been up early as the door to the barn was open and the riding mower was in front of the cabin.

"Good morning, Martin. Thanks for coming. It's going to take quite a while to get this place in shape. I looked through the barn and this mower seems to be in pretty good condition, at least I didn't have too much trouble getting it started. After the grounds are cleaned up, you might want to go through the barn and start clearing out all the stuff in there. But, I'm sure it will take a few months to get everything organized.

"I'm going back to New York for a few weeks," Franz said, as he handed Martin a slip of paper with his name and phone number on it. If you need to get a hold of me just call this number. I had the phone connected in the cabin and you can just use that. I set up accounts at the lumber mill and the Edwardton Hardware store in case you need to get anything. I told them to just let you sign for any purchases and I would take care of it when I get back to Mercyville. Oh, yes, I almost forgot. Here's a key to the cabin."

"It seems as though you have everything taken care of. What do you want me to do with the things in the barn?" Martin asked.

"Keep anything you feel you might need to use around here. I took a quick look around and there's nothing I want to keep. If there is anything you want, just take it. A lot of odds and ends were sold at the auction so I don't think there should be too much left. I'll be leaving shortly for New York, so I'll just leave everything in your hands," Franz said.

As he reached in his pocket, he pulled out his wallet and handed Martin six-hundred dollars.

"This should take care of our salary until I get back," he said.

As Martin watched Franz's car pull out of the driveway, he couldn't help but think of the strange twist of events. Two years ago he was chasing Tom Aaron over the mountains and now he was caretaker of his property. Even though Franz Kohler was now the owner of the homestead, to Martin it would always be known as "the Aaron Place". Today he would begin his unsolicited employment as Franz Kohler's caretaker. Things were looking up he thought, as he started mowing down the remnants of the past.

It was noon as Charles and Paul Devon stood looking at the new sprawling building at the end of the Devon property closed to the road. On the front of the lawn was a large white sign with black lettering that read: Paul Devon, DVM, Endless Mountain Veterinary Clinic. It was a long hard struggle, but Paul Devon was now Paul Devon, doctor of veterinary medicine. This had been his dream ever since he was a child. Charles had given his son this beautiful, fully equipped, clinic as a graduation gift. After Paul's riding accident, Charles had put this day out of his mind. He never believed Paul's dream would come true but then he thought he had been wrong before.

From Paul's clinic he could see the Aarons' cabin a half-mile down the road, and as with Martin, it always brought back memories of the kidnappings.

As the Devons stood in front of the clinic, a car pulled in to the parking lot. A young man got out holding a mixed-breed canine. Paul walked over to him and asked if he could help. The young man explained that the dog had run in front of his car and he could not avoid hitting him. The new Dr. Devon had his first patient.

As Paul examined the dog, the only major damage to him were a few minor cuts on the leg. The dog appeared to be a stray and looked like he needed a good meal and a bath.

Paul asked the young man if he wanted to keep the dog and he said no. He was just passing through Mercyville on his way back to college; but he would pay the dog's medical bill. When the college student left, Paul put the nameless dog in the kennel, along with food and water.

"Well," Paul said to the dog, as he watched him devour the food. "Maybe it was destiny you were hit. If it weren't for that young man, you would have died of starvation in a day or two. A couple of day's rests and some decent food should put you in good shape."

As he stood outside, next to the kennel, he could hear the sound of the mower going over at the former Aaron homestead. He was at the auction yesterday and introduced himself to his new neighbor, Franz Kohler. Paul thought it would be interesting living next door to an art dealer. His parents loved art and antiques and were anxious to meet this Mr. Kohler.

The Devon property and the, now, Kohler property met in the middle of a thick grove of hemlocks. There was never a reason to fence off the perimeter of his land although Charles had thought about it after the kidnappings. Of course, a fence would not have stopped what had happened at West Knob.

The ring of the phone broke Paul's thoughts. It was Sam Sell, the owner of a large dairy farm. One of his bovines had become lame and he needed Paul to come out to the farm.

When Paul left the clinic, he passed Kohler's cabin and could see that Martin Benson was mowing the overgrowth. He thought, at least it would be good to see the place cleaned up and have someone living there again. Practically anyone would be better than the Aaron brothers.

Paul was almost to the Sell farm when his cell phone rang.

"Dr.Devon here," he said.

"Well, hello, Dr. Devon," a cheerful female voice replied. It was Paul's wife Suzanne.

"I just got back from town. I'm sorry I'm late, but the errands took a little longer than I expected. I'm over at the clinic and I see you have your first patient! I'll stay here until you get back. I'll talk to you later," she said and hung up the phone.

Suzanne had been Paul's speech therapist after the accident and over the months, they had fallen in love. They had been married almost two years during which time Paul completed Veterinary College. They were living temporarily at West Knob while their new home was being built. They were both glad to be finished with college and were anxious to be moving into their own home.

Their house was being built on the property at West Knob. It sat on an open plateau overlooking the valley. Like West Knob, it was a two-story stone house. It had a large portico extending out over part of a circular driveway. The interior was rustic with a colonial flare and large open beam ceilings. The house was situated so the mountains and valley could be viewed from every room in the house. Paul had named the house White Deer Point, after a pure white buck that frequented West Knob. He had seen the buck on numerous occasions and looked to him as a symbol of good luck. From Paul's viewpoint, the deer had brought him good fortune in his recovery from the riding accident. Everything seemed to be looking up for the Devon family, although they would never get over the untimely death of Joseph.

For the last four hours, Martin Benson had been mowing his way through the past two years of unkempt grass. At least he had put a dent in to what seemed like a never-ending task. He pulled the mower up in front of the cabin and stopped to take a break. As he started up the steps of the cabin, he saw the corner of what appeared to be a wallet sticking out from under the bottom of the step. He reached down, brushed away the dirt, and gave the object a tug. It was a wallet, or what was left of a man's wallet. When he opened it, some of the dried leather fell to the ground. Inside there was a plastic covered driver's license. He went in to the cabin and with a wet cloth tried to wipe the dirt off of the I.D. The license belonged to a William Meredith from Edwardton. Martin thought that he had heard the name but he wasn't sure. He laid the wallet on the kitchen counter and got himself a cold drink from the refrigerator.

It seemed uncomfortable being in the Aarons' cabin and he had the feeling that the brothers were still there. He stepped back out on the porch and surveyed what he had accomplished so far. Well, he thought, maybe it wouldn't take as long as he first surmised to get Franz's property back in shape. A wide swath of the lawn had been cut with about three times that much let to get through. Martin had a definite fear of snakes, poisonous or not, and hated going into the high grass. He decided to get everything mowed down, as soon as possible and then he would start on clearing out the barn.

At four o'clock, he put the mower back in the barn, locked up the cabin and headed home. He had put in a good first day and hoped the Aaron brothers would appreciate his efforts to recover the homestead from the point of disaster.

As he drove up his private driveway, he thought about the wallet with the William Meredith driver's license. Somewhere, floating around in his mind, he remembered hearing the name, but the information had not landed in the recall section of his thoughts. Tomorrow he would think about that. Tonight the venison stayed in the springhouse; tonight was chicken night.

11

The young Dr. Devon was opening up his clinic when Martin Benson drove by heading in the direction of town.

It was eight-thirty when Martin walked in to the country store/post office. He had gotten gas for the mower and came inside to pay for it. The usual morning crowd of the conclave of opinion makers was slowing drifting in and taking a place at the oversized round table. The always on coffeepot had been replaced by a coffee machine that dispensed a variety of caffeine loaded favors which included French Vanilla, Irish Cream, Hazelnut and for the more adventurous taste buds, Cappuccino was available.

Matt Wallace arrived just as Martin was paying for the gasoline.

"Good morning Martin," he said. "How about having a cup of coffee with us?"

"Thanks, Mr. Wallace, but I'm working for Mr. Kohler out at the old Aaron place. I need to stay with it. Mr. Kohler is coming back in a few weeks and I want it to look nice when he gets here," Martin said. "Maybe another time."

Matt thought that was the about the longest conversation anyone in town had ever had with Martin. It seemed as though he was slowly melding into the populace of Mercyville.

Driving back to Franz's place, Martin thought he would take a break from the mowing and look over the assortment of odds and ends in the barn. There were years of stuff thrown haphazardly in the lower level of the barn and the loft didn't seem to be in any better shape. From the looks of the loft, it appeared that birds had made one corner of it as a seasonal nesting place.

When Martin opened the barn door, a raccoon made its way outside. He had no idea what other surprises were in store for him inside of the barn. "I think this is going to take a lot longer than the outside of the property to straighten out," he said to himself.

Slowly, he started moving crates with gardening equipment, old hunting magazines, an assortment of old clothes and endless boxes of newspapers and old paper work. When he had cleared away the seemingly worthless junk, at the bottom of the pile he found a large size dog kennel that appeared to be in good shape, at least it would be when the years of dust was removed. He thought he would give the kennel to Dr. Devon, as he could probably put it to good use. Martin had made his first decision on the departure of an item from the array of miscellaneous junk.

Coming into view, there were tables, chairs, beds, boxes of camping equipment and a stack of old fishing rods. It suddenly occurred to Martin that the only thing that had been recently removed from the barn was the riding mower. He thought he had better think seriously as to how he was going to get rid of all of the Aarons' dust-covered belongings.

After careful thought, he decided to put the give-away items in one section, the un-useable in another and the things the thought Mr. Franz might want to keep in another area. At least Martin was making decisions outside of the perimeters of his own property.

Two hours later, a small area of the barn had been cleared for the keep items. He had pulled a burn barrel to the outside of the barn and started throwing in the obsolete paper work, old magazines and a variety of pieces of wood. This is a nightmare, he thought, but if I take it a little bit at a time I think I can organize it before Mr. Franz gets back.

Two hours were about all Martin could take in the dust-filled clutter of almost useless items. He got on the mower and continued to extend the swath of already cut grass. At least outside he could breathe the fresh air.

It was nearing four o'clock and Martin decided to call it a day. On his way home, he would stop by Dr. Devon's Clinic and drop off the dog kennel. At least it was a usable item. He locked the barn, put the kennel in the back of his truck and headed for the clinic.

Sleigh bells on the front door of the office rang as Martin entered the clinic, carrying the kennel. A moment later, Dr. Devon appeared and welcomed him.

"Dr. Devon, I thought that you might be able to use this dog kennel. Mr. Franz said to get rid of all the stuff in the barn and I thought of you," Martin said.

"That was very thoughtful of you. I certainly will find use for it. You can never have too many kennels in a clinic like this," Dr. Devon said.

Just then a huge ball of black, brown and white fur came running from the back of clinic and around the corner of the desk. All excited and wagging his tail, he ran over to Martin.

"That's a friendly dog you have there. Does he belong to you?" Martin asked.

"Well, not exactly," the doctor said. "A young man hit him with his car and brought him here to be treated. Fortunately, he wasn't hurt very bad. I think he was a stray, as he was close to dying of starvation. I'm amazed at how well these animals respond to a bath, food and a little love. He didn't have a collar, so I don't even know his name or where he came from.

"Martin, you wouldn't want a nice dog, would you? I've given him all of his shots and checked him over and he seems to be in good shape. He certainly seems friendly toward you. I think he would make a great companion," Dr. Devon said.

The nameless dog had lain at Martin's feet and was looking up at him with that, "Please take me home look".

"What would I have to pay for him?" Martin asked.

"Not a thing, Martin," Dr. Devon said. " We could call it a trade for the kennel and I'll even throw in a forty-pound bag of dog food and a collar."

The nameless canine kept staring up at Martin as if to say, "Please say yes."

"Ok, Dr. Devon, it's a deal. When do you want me to pick him up?" Martin asked.

"You can take him with you right now if you like," Dr. Devon said.

Martin leaned over and patted the dog on the head. With one touch, the deal was settled. Martin had a companion and the stray dog had found a home.

Dr. Devon went in the back of his office and came back with a red collar and a huge bag of dog food. As he put the collar on the dog he could not help but think how much fate plays a part in life.

"Let's load him up. I'll put the food in the back of your truck," Dr. Devon said.

As they pulled out of the clinic parking lot, the nameless dog had his head hanging out of the truck window and his long ears began flapping in the breeze. Indeed it was a good day, Paul thought, as he watched the new companions drive down the road headed for a life of new adventures.

When Martin pulled up in front of his gate, he could see some of the wood he stacked up for sale was gone. There was an envelope stuck in the gated. When he opened it, he found a ten-dollar bill and a note saying they had taken some wood for camping and hoped the ten dollars would cover the cost. To Martin, it was twice as much as he would have charged. Indeed it was a good day!

As he and his nameless friend entered his cabin, the dog sniffed all around, then went over and lay down next to the wood stove.

"I'm going to have to think of a name for you," he said to the sleeping dog.

Now the cabin was no longer a house, now it was a home. As Martin looked at the dog, his nameless friend was no longer without a name. With a large brown patch over his left eye, Martin decided to call him Patch.

There was less than a week and a half before Franz Kohler would be back to his second home in Mercyville.

Martin had worked feverishly on the grounds and the barn. All the while he worked, Patch explored the grounds or slept on the cabin's porch; never letting Martin out of his sight.

So far Martin had cleared out more that half of the barn. To get rid of some of the barn's paraphernalia he set it out front of the cabin next to the road and put a Free Stuff sign on it. All day long vehicles stopped and people took whatever they wanted from the array of goods. This seemed to Martin to be a pretty good way of clearing out the barn. At least some people could find a way to put the old relics to use. He figured a few more Free Stuff days and he would have the barn pretty well cleared out.

He had now worked his way to the back of the barn where there was a stack of miscellaneous chairs, a large round barrel base table, a four drawer bureau, several old trunks and a pile of what appeared to be antique frames mixed in with some garden equipment.

He put the chairs out front in the Free Stuff pile along with two of the empty trunks. The chairs were being taken faster than he could bring them from the barn. It seemed as though the word had spread around Mercyville of the Free Stuff sign at the former Aarons' place.

Inside of the barn, Martin opened the third trunk and found a stack of old newspapers. Among the papers, he found a hunting license with the name of William Meredith. Opening up one of the old newspapers, he saw an article on a missing hunter by the name of William Meredith. Now it was all coming back to him as his brain stopped on recall. The wallet must have belonged to the same man, but what was it doing at the Aarons' place? It all seemed rather strange to him. He put the license and the newspapers on the barrel table and carried the empty trunk out to the dwindling pile of give-away items.

The barn was pretty well cleaned out except for the frames, which he was keeping for Mr. Franz, the garden equipment, bureau and round table. He thought that he would keep the bureau and table for himself to use in his cabin. The only thing left to do was clean out the loft. When that was finished, he could clear some downed trees on the edge of the property.

Little by little, the Kohler homestead was revived. With the mammoth grounds now manicured, Martin could visualize a new house on the property. With the overgrowth cleared away, even the barn looked good. He was pleased with what he had accomplished and he hoped that Mr. Franz would approve of his efforts.

He had put in a full day and was ready to go home. Patch must have sensed it was time to leave and went running off of the porch toward Martin. He had one more thing to do and that was to put the table and the chest in his truck. He backed his truck up to the barn and loaded both pieces of the furniture. It took all of his strength to load the heavy table.

All the way home, Patch kept his head out of the window, letting the cool breeze blow in his face.

When he arrived home, he took the furniture off of the truck and put it in his cabin. It had been a long day and both he and Patch were glad to be back at the cabin. Tomorrow is another day, he thought.

For the next few days, Martin continued to clean out the barn's loft. He came across more old chairs, a dusty pile of blankets, boxes of broken dishes, an assortment of old pots and pans, several pairs of fishing waders, half-full paint cans and a small cast iron stove. The stove was small enough to add to his cabin, so he thought he would keep it. With the exception of the paint cans, everything would go out to the Free Stuff area. After that was done, the barn would be in shape for a more practicable storage arrangement. He thought he would put up hooks to hold the lawn and garden tools and the garden hoses. The cleared out barn could now hold several cars or trucks.

As he was putting the last assortment of Free Stuff out front, Dr. Devon stopped by and inquired about his new dog. Martin, who seldom smiled, was beaming from ear to ear talking about his recently named friend.

"He's a really good dog, Dr. Devon but Patch acts strange in my cabin ever since I brought home the new table and bureau. He won't go near either one. Something must have scared him, I guess," Martin said.

"It takes time for dogs to get used to anything new that comes in to his territory or their familiar surroundings. He'll be all right. Just give him a little time. I'm glad that it's all working out for you and Patch," Dr. Devon said.

With the barn finished, he could concentrate on the downed trees. He brought along his chain saw and thought that it wouldn't take long to cut them up for firewood. Martin was an expert at tree cutting and began to breeze through the trees. When he was finished he would stack the logs on the porch of the cabin to use in the fireplace.

After an hour of cutting, Martin decided he would quit for the day. Everything was finished except the wood cutting and he had a few days to get that done before Mr. Franz arrived.

When Martin arrived home, he and Patch went to the springhouse where he took out a package of venison to add to the dog's dinner. Patch liked to go to the springhouse and stand in the cold water as it ran through the building. He did the same thing every time he went there.

After dinner, Martin and his companion sat outside of the cabin. Periodically, Patch would spot a squirrel and give chase to the furry creature, which he never could catch.

Life was certainly looking up for Martin and now he had a good reason to get up each morning.

Patch woke Martin up early and wanted to go outside. Reluctantly, he got out of bed and let him out. Well, thought Martin, since I'm up, I might as well put on a pot of coffee. While the coffee was brewing, he dressed and straightened up the cabin. The top of the round barrel table seemed a little loose so Martin thought he would fix it before going out to Franz's. With the large barrel base and the thick wood top, it was very heavy, even for him. He turned it on its side, got out his drill and started removing the old screws.

As he removed the last screw, the heavy top came off. When Martin moved the top, an unimaginable thing happened. He stood frozen in place and for a few seconds he thought he must have been imagining what he was witnessing. This couldn't be possible. His mind was racing and his heart was pounding as he thought it was just a bad dream. He wanted to scream but he couldn't and his body started to shake as he stared at the human skull and bones that had rolled out of the barrel and on to the floor. All he could think of was getting away from the cabin and going any place; any place but where he was. He threw open the cabin door just as Patch was about to come in and ran over to his truck.

When he opened the truck door, the now excited canine jumped in before him. Getting away was all he could think of. He started driving like a maniac down the winding mountain road and on one sharp curve; Patch slid clear across the seat and landed hard against Martin.

The only place he could think of to go was the country store.

As he approached the store, he barely missed hitting the gas pump and luckily hit the concrete barrier. He jumped out of the truck, which was left awkwardly parked in front of the gas pump and ran in to the store. A few of the conclave of opinion makers had heard the crash and jumped up from the round table.

As Martin fled to the security of the store, the men could not believe what could be wrong. He was ghost white and visibly shaking.

"Martin, what's wrong?" Matt Wallace asked.

Martin wanted to talk, but he was shaking so badly, nothing would come out of his mouth. The men guided him over to the chair and made him sit down.

"Martin, Martin, it's ok! We're all here. Calm down and tell us what happened?" Matt said.

One of the men of the conclave got him a glass of water. By now, the ladies who worked at the store had come over to the round table and were looking at Martin. After a few minutes, they had succeeded in calming him down enough so he was able to talk.

'It's awful, it's awful," was all he could say.

"Martin, Martin, tell us what's so awful?" Matt tried to pry it out of him.

"The head that rolled out on my cabin floor. Oh, my God, it's awful," he said.

Everyone just stared at each other hoping they hadn't heard right what he said.

"Martin, we have to go back there and look at what's happened," Matt said.

"No, no!" Martin screamed. "I'm not going back there!"

"I'm going to have to go out there and see what has happened," Matt said.

"I'll go with you," one of the opinion makers said.

"Keep Martin here and keep him calm until we get back," Matt said.

12

Matt Wallace had no idea what he would find when he reached Martin's cabin. From the state he was in when he came in to the store, it was obvious that it couldn't be anything good.

When they reached the driveway they pulled up close to the cabin. Slowly, Matt opened the door to the cabin and they both stepped inside. They could see why Martin was in a near state of shock. A human skull, jawbone and several fragments of bone were lying on the floor next to the wooden tabletop. Matt pushed the top away from the barrel base and was stunned to see what appeared to be a full skeleton with shreds of clothing inside of the barrel. Both Matt and the opinion maker had to turn away from the gruesome sight. Neither man could totally comprehend what they were witnessing.

"Let's get out of here," Matt said. "We have to call the police right away. No wonder Martin didn't want to come back here. How the Devil did all of this happen? He must have been totally petrified when that skull rolled out of the barrel!"

Matt stepped outside to his truck, got his cell phone out and called the police. He explained as much as he knew about the horrible event and told them he would wait at Martin's cabin until they got there. He told them that Martin was at the country store in Mercyville.

In about ten minutes, the police arrived at Martin's home. Two other officers had been dispatched to the country store to talk to Martin.

The officers' put up yellow tape around the perimeters of Martin's cabin where the long deceased lay rolled out on Martin's braided rug.

Shortly, a police photographer arrived and began taking pictures of the interior of Martin's home. They had called the Coroner and he said he would be there within a half-hour. Matt and the opinion maker just stood outside and shook their heads in disbelief.

Back at the country store, the shaken Martin tried to explain everything that had happened and how he had gotten the barrel table from the Aarons' place. He told them about William Meredith's wallet and the newspaper clippings. This was the only connection that he could fathom at the moment. Truthfully, in his present state of mind, he wasn't sure about too much. One of the conclave men had gone out and moved Martin's truck and brought Patch in to the store. Even with all of the commotion, he remained calm and had fallen asleep at Martin's feet.

The cashier at the store gave him a cup of coffee and slowly the color was returning to his ashen face.

"Mr. Benson, I just want to make sure I have this all right. You said you got the barrel table from the Aarons' barn. What did you do with the wallet and the newspapers?" the officer asked.

"I put them on the kitchen counter at Aarons' cabin," he said, still shaking. "I also found a hunting license with the name William Meredith on it and I put that on the counter too."

"Mr. Benson, will you ride along with us back to your cabin?" the Officer asked.

"I can't go back there. I just can't go back there. It's too horrible!" Martin said.

"You don't have to get out of the car. If you like, you and your dog can stay in the patrol car until the scene is cleaned up," the officer said.

Reluctantly, Martin went along, with his dog, and got in the back seat of the car.

As they arrived at his home, he could see the yellow crime scene tape stretched around the door and the dog jumped out and started running all around. Matt saw Martin in the car and went over to see how he was holding up.

"How are you doing, Martin?" Matt asked.

"Not very well. I don't want to see that barrel and them bones again. It's all too awful, Mr. Wallace," he replied.

Matt pitied Martin. He was finally coming out of his shell and becoming a part of the Mercyville village, then this had to happen. I can understand why he was so terrified and why he doesn't want to go inside. It would have been a shock to anyone when that skull rolled out of the barrel.

The opinion maker walked over to the car where Martin was still sitting and spoke to him. "I put one of your chairs over there near that hemlock. I think you might be more comfortable over there."

Martin hesitated, but got out of the car and went over to the chair. Patch saw him and followed close behind.

The Coroner had just arrived, ducked under the yellow tape and went inside. A half-hour later he came out with one of the officers and they were carrying a body bag. Two other officers were carrying the tabletop and the barrel. They loaded the dismantled table in to the crime scene truck and put the body bag in the van marked Coroner.

A State Trooper walked over to where Martin was sitting.

"Mr. Benson, I hate to do this to you, but I need you to come along with us out to the Aarons' cabin. You'll have to show us where the barrel table and the other things were found. I assume you have a key to the cabin."

"Yes, I have a key." He reached in his pocket and pulled out a key. All the stuff I found is in the cabin on the kitchen counter," Martin volunteered.

The State Troopers, Martin and Patch drove the six miles over to the former Aarons' place. Martin unlocked the cabin door, went inside and showed them where the wallet and other things were. While they were still inside, the crime scene unit pulled up next to the parked patrol car. They went in to the cabin and removed the wallet, newspapers and the hunting license. After they were finished, they asked Martin to take them to the barn and show them where the barrel table had been stored.

As the group walked to the barn, Patch ran along next to Martin. For Patch, this was just another day but for his master, it was the worst day of his life. He wondered how he could have gotten involved in the whole darn disaster. He didn't cause anyone any trouble and here he was in the center of a murder case he knew nothing about. It would take a long time for him to get over this unfortunate event.

Martin opened the barn door and showed the officers where the barrel table had stood. They wouldn't find any other evidence in here, they thought. The barn was surgically clean, thanks to Martin. Two Troopers went to the loft, but like the floor level of the barn, if there had been any evidence, Martin unknowingly had eliminated it when he cleaned the barn. The only place something might be found was in the burn barrel, which luckily, he had not gotten around to burning.

The men of the crime unit took the whole burn barrel and put it in their truck. The photographer was now taking pictures of the almost empty barn and the immaculately manicured grounds.

Back at Martin's homestead, Matt and the opinion maker, with the permission of the Coroner, tried to clean up the desecrated sanctuary he called home. Matt wondered how Martin would ever feel comfortable there again. They both felt terrible about what he had unwittingly became involved in. All anyone could do for him now was to be supportive and keep him in the perimeter of the caring people of Mercyville.

The Troopers and the Coroner had finished their search of both the Aarons and the Benson's properties. They wanted to drive Martin home but he asked them to take him to the store so he could get his truck. A conclave member had moved the fender-dented truck away from the gas pump and put it in a more obscure spot. Word of the whole episode had spread quickly through the village. It looked as though the Plain-Jane town of Mercyville was back on the map of strange events.

The lumber mill foreman was at the store when the police arrived with Martin and offered to drive his truck back to his place for him. Martin was mentally drained and took him up on the offer. One of the store clerks followed behind them. When they got to his cabin, Matt and the opinion maker were still there.

Matt asked Martin if he wanted him to stay with him for the night?

"Mr. Wallace, I just need to be alone. I don't want to talk to anybody. This whole day has been like another bad dream," he said. "I feel just like I did when them kidnappings took place. Them Aarons are still causing trouble even if they are in jail. I think that place of their's has nothing but bad things happening there."

The men didn't want to leave Martin by himself, but if he wanted to be alone, there was nothing more they could do now.

As everyone left, Martin and Patch were once again behind the now not-so-secure perimeters of his fence.

Two hours had passed, when there was a knock at the cabin door. Martin, still shaken from the whole experience, hesitantly opened it. To his surprise, it was Charles Devon.

"Martin, we heard about the predicament you unfortunately became involved in. Rebecca made dinner and a pie for you. If there is anything we can do for you, or if there is anything you need, please let us know. Our doors at West Knob are always open to you," Charles said.

"Thank you, Mr. Devon, but I think Patch and I will be all right for now," he said.

As he closed the door, Martin began to think about how much the people of the village really cared about him. For Martin, this was a whole new way of thinking.

Two days had passed since the skull and barrel incident. The police had searched the grounds and cabin of Franz Kohler but they had found nothing they felt suspicious in relationship to what had already happened. They had asked Martin to call them if he found anything out of the ordinary. He could not possibly comprehend what could be more out of the ordinary than a skull rolling across your kitchen floor. Just the thought of going back to Franz's made his stomach turn upside down. In four days Franz would be back and he still had the downed trees to cut up and stack on the porch. He was wishing the work was finished and he wouldn't have to go over there again. He wondered what Franz would think when he hears about what happened. But, he had paid him for three weeks work and he thought it only fair that he hold up his end of the deal.

Since he found the skull, or maybe it should be said, the skull found him, sleeping had been difficult. Even with Patch there, he was feeling very insecure about being in his own home. The same nightmare of the skull rolling out of the barrel played over and over in his mind as if the recall button in his brain was stuck. If only it would stop, he thought.

Patch had been outside early in the morning and now he was barking to come back in. Martin opened the door and the happy canine trotted inside. He thought he had to pull himself together, if not for himself, at least for Patch.

Slowly, he dressed, fed Patch and straightened up his cabin. To look at Martin, you wouldn't think he would be an organized man, but to the contrary, he had a place for everything and he liked everything in its place. It actually upset him if something was misplaced.

He took a deep breath and called Patch to go with him. Against his better judgment, he was going to Franz's to finish what he had promised to do.

Unlike two days ago when he drove crazily down the mountain, today he drove slowly hoping something would occur to deter him from getting there. Patch seemed to enjoy the slow ride and stood up on the front seat with his head out of the window and his ears blowing in the breeze.

As he was passing Dr. Devon's Clinic, he saw the doctor getting out of his car. The young doctor saw Martin and motioned for him to stop. He pulled into the parking lot and Paul walked over to his truck. Patch remembered Paul and he began wagging his tail and barking as he approached the vehicle.

"Good morning, Martin. I heard about what happened to you and I just wanted you to know that I'm here if I can do anything for you. I stopped over to Franz's yesterday but I didn't see you," Paul said.

"No, Dr. Devon, I was too upset to come back. But, I promised Franz that I'd get everything done. I'm almost finished though. We both thought it would have taken much longer, but once I got started, it all went pretty fast," Martin said.

"It looks as though you and Patch have bonded well. He's really a handsome dog and very good-natured. I don't think there could have been a better match than you and Patch," Paul said.

"You know, Dr.Devon, I was thinking about how Patch wouldn't go near the barrel table I took home. Do you think he knew something was wrong with it?" Martin asked.

"I can't say for sure, but animals seem to have an extra sense that we don't have. Dogs and cats are very sensitive to many things we really aren't even aware of. There are many cases of them doing extraordinary things. We'll never know for sure, but for myself, I listen to the animals. There is a lot they can teach us," Dr. Devon said.

I better get over to Franz's and get to work. I want everything to look good when he gets here." remarked Martin.

As they drove away, Paul thought how fortunate it was that Patch came into Martin's life when he did. It seems as though that the right thing happens at just the right time.

Martin started cutting through the last of the downed tree, as Patch surveyed the mowed perimeters of Franz's property. If ever a dog fell in to canine heaven, it was Patch. He had found a good home, had plenty of food, a great companion and the freedom to roam. A poor, almost dead stray, had become the lottery winner in the world of dogs.

Martin had cut up the one downed tree, split the wood and stacked it on the porch of the cabin. Franz hadn't asked him to but he thought he would clean up the cabin. The kitchen closets were devoid of any recent canned or packaged food so the thought he would pick up a few basic supplies in Edwardton to tide Franz over until he settled in.

The bookcase was still piled high with an assortment of books and miscellaneous pieces of pottery. The bookcase that once stood in front of the loft door was now in its original place. It was up in the loft that the Aarons had kept the kidnapped women. As he was taking the items off of the shelf to be cleaned, another bad memory drifted through his mind.

Several hours later, the cabin began to take on a crisper look. In the kitchen, he threw out all of the old, dust-covered canned goods, removed the blankets from the beds and shook them out, polished the furniture, scrubbed the kitchen floor and vacuumed the braided rugs. At least it would be clean when Franz arrived, Martin thought.

Martin started to realize that the more he worked the less he thought about all of the terrible events that had happened. His brain was going off of replay and now slid into the intermittent zone.

As he looked around the cabin, he was pleased with the progress he had made in bringing it back to life. Tomorrow he would go to Edwardton and pick up a few necessities. It would feel go to get away from Mercyville even for a couple of hours. Since he was no longer a collector of warning signs, it won't be necessary to stop at the Edwardton Hardware store tomorrow. He would go directly to the grocery store and then get back to Franz's cabin.

Patch waited in the truck while inside of the store he stacked his shopping cart with soups, canned stews, tuna, crackers, coffee, tea and several refrigerator items. He wasn't used to shopping in a large grocery store, being a simple man; his only requirements were meat and potatoes. The few items he needed, he picked up at the country store in Mercyville. The variety of food products in the grocery store made his head swim! When he passed the meat counter, there were several bags of big bones marked Free, so he took one bag for Patch. His cart was now near the overload mark so he decided to check out. If there was anything Franz wanted, he could pick it up for him later.

Back at the almost surgically clean cabin, he arranged the groceries on the shelves and put the perishables in the refrigerator. With that finished, he walked out on the porch and sipped a cold cola. Soft drinks were something he seldom indulged in, but today it was hot and the cold drink satisfied his thirst.

He had given Patch one of the large free bones and was watching him bury it for future consumption. He wondered why he had waited so long to get another dog, but then he thought he must have just been waiting for Patch to come along.

It was eleven o'clock Friday morning and Martin was just finishing cutting up the last downed tree when a car pulled up in front of Franz's cabin. Two men got out of the car and walked up on the porch. Martin stopped his work and as he walked toward the cabin, he could see that it was Franz Kohler.

"Good morning. I didn't think that I was at the right place," Franz said.

"Martin, I'd like you to meet my architect, Carl Winslow. Carl, this is my caretaker, Martin Benson," Franz said.

"I never expected this place to look so good! I can hardly believe you accomplished all of this in three weeks!" Franz said.

"Well, Mr. Kohler, once I got started I just kept going. It was easier than I first thought it would be. I cleared everything out of the barn and yesterday I cleaned up the cabin. I bought a few groceries and stocked the kitchen shelves for you," Martin said.

Jokingly, Franz asked, "Is there anything you didn't think of ?"

There's one thing I have to tell you that happened here while you were away."

Franz and Carl pulled up two of the porch chairs and sat down.

Martin was glad they were seated as he related the whole episode leading up to the barrel incident at this cabin. Franz couldn't believe what he was hearing.

"Do the police have any idea who that person was you found?" Franz asked with a look of concern on his face.

"They didn't say anything. They just took the barrel table, the skeleton and that stuff I found with that William Meredith name on it. They even took the burn barrel," Martin replied.

"To say the least, this is certainly a terrible thing that happened. If I would have known anything like that was around here, I would have had the police here right away. I'm sorry you had to go through all of that. I hope it won't make you change your mind about working here?" Franz said.

At first I didn't want to come back here, but when I did come back and started working again, I felt a little better," Martin admitted.

Just then, Patch came running around the corner of the cabin and up on the porch.

"This is Patch. Dr. Devon gave him to me. He said he needed a good home, so I took him. He's a real good dog. I take him everyplace with me," the proud owner said.

"Let's walk down and take a look at the barn," Franz said. "From the outside, it looks a lot different from what I saw when I left three weeks ago. Looks like this old barn has some good bones."

As soon as he said it, Martin just stared at him with strange look on his face.

"I'm sorry, Martin. What I meant by that was that the barn has a good, sound structure. I certainly picked the wrong words," Franz apologized.

Martin had never heard that expression before and didn't know what it meant until Franz explained it to him. Martin didn't think any bones were good, at least not in his book. The only bones he ever wanted to be involved with were the ones he had gotten for Patch.

He opened the barn door and all three went inside.

"Martin, how did you get rid of everything that was in here?" Franz questioned.

Martin proudly proceeded to explain his Free Stuff merchandising campaign. Being from New York City, Franz and Carl had never heard of the Free Stuff plan but whatever worked they thought was good enough for them.

"Where was the barrel table setting?" asked Franz.

Martin pointed to the area where the table had been setting. After Martin's cleaning frenzy, there was no visible evidence of any misguided deeds of the past. Detergent, bleach, suds and scrub bubbles, scouring powder and hot water had sterilized the former crime scene.

"I saved those picture frames over there. They were underneath of a pile of old chairs. I thought you might want to use them. I kept all of the lawn and garden tools too," Martin said.

Franz was impressed with Martin's neatness and organizational skills.

"I certainly would like to thank you for all you have done. I didn't expect all of this, especially now that I know all you have been though," Franz said.

As soon as we unload the car, Carl and I are going to pick out the best site for the house.

When Franz went into the cabin, he was immediately surprised with the cleaning and tidying up of his new second home. I was lucky to have found Martin, he thought, and I'm not letting him get away.

The two men started searching for the best location for the house. Pointing to his right, Franz suggested a spot that would lookout over the Mercyville valley. After an hour of looking over several more locations, Carl agreed that his first choice would be the most suitable. Carl had been in contact with a large construction company in Edwardton and they were ready to break ground as soon a decision was made on the site. This afternoon, Carl and Franz would go to Edwardton and finalize the plans for the house. Franz hoped it would be completed by the fall.

With the building at West Knob and now with the start of Franz's house, the face of the landscape of Mercyville was slowly changing.

13

Martin had taken the four-drawer bureau, which he had gotten from Franz's barn, outside his cabin. Today he would sanitize it as only he could do.

When he was finished with his rub and scrub method, the grains of the cherry wood shone as well as the day it was made. Even the ironstone knobs glistened in the sunlight. He put the bureau back in the corner of his cabin and the rejuvenated piece of furniture seemed to add an air of elegance to his humble homestead.

From the shelf, with the canned goods on it, he took down a metal box, opened it up and took out a small gold-framed picture of his parents. It was the only picture he had of them. Looking at the picture, suppressed memories flooded back into his mind of a not so happy childhood. His mother died when he was ten years old. His father was an alcoholic and drifted in and out of his life for as long as he could remember. Early in his youth, he learned to fend for himself. His father would leave for days at a time but eventually he would stagger back home. He was eighteen the last time he saw his father. It didn't matter to him one way or another if he did or didn't see his father. After a month had passed, he knew for sure that he was on his own for good and never bothered to report him missing.

On top of the scrubbed and polished bureau, Martin placed the gold-framed picture, the only remnant of his mother and father.

The summer passed quickly and the construction of the Franz Kohler house was progressing rapidly.

Martin went over to Franz's several times a week. He kept up with the mowing and had started going through the surrounding hemlock forest clearing the downed trees. With so much wood, it would keep Franz supplied for a number of years. He even started stacking it in the infamous barn with good bones.

One day, Martin found out from one of Franz's neighbors, that his beloved Patch, was not the good boy he thought he was. The tri-colored, once homeless stray, was going to be a father. The neighbor wasn't at all pleased about the union of a stray and her pure-breed poodle. Martin hated to do it, but as soon as he could make an appointment with Dr. Devon, Patch was going to have to lose a portion of his lower anatomy. Martin thought if Patch wanted to continue to be a free spirit, the canine had an obligation to at least be responsible.

Early the next morning Martin was waiting for Dr. Devon as he opened up the clinic. When he had unlocked the door, Martin walked in with a leash on Patch.

"Is something wrong with Patch?" he asked Martin, with a puzzled look on his face.

"No, there isn't anything wrong with him, but Franz's neighbor, the one with the white poodle, is pretty mad at him. She said Patch was going to be a father and her poodle is the mother. I think, Dr. Devon, you're going to have to do something to him. I don't want the neighbors to be mad at Patch or me."

Dr. Devon laughed and shook his finger at Patch. "I thought you were a good boy and now I'm hearing this story about you being a lover. Well, Boy, I'm going to have to eliminate a little bit of your amorous side!" he said.

"Martin, I'll take him today and you can stop by tomorrow afternoon and pick him up. Don't worry, he'll be fine," young Dr. Devon said.

"How much is this going to cost?" Martin asked.

"If it's ok with you, Martin, I'd like to propose a trade. Occasionally, when I go out on large animal calls, I can use an extra hand. You seem to be just the right person to handle the job. What do you think about that?" Dr. Devon asked.

Martin was thrilled with the offer. To him, working beside Dr. Devon was something he never imagined.

"I like the idea. I like that a lot!" Martin said.

His only concern now was Patch and he hoped his best friend wouldn't be too mad at him!

Over at West Knob, the Devon house had once again turned into a home of joy. Even though Charles and Rebecca thought of their late son, Joseph, everyday, they finally had some happy events to look forward to.

After his accident, having Paul finish college and open up his own veterinary clinic was far beyond any of their expectations.

Not only had Joseph left his legacy of two beautiful grandsons, they just found out that Suzanne was expecting their first child around Christmas.

Over the past two years, Paula O'Brien had made frequent visits to West Knob with the twins. Especially for the boys, Charles had put in a swimming pool and a beautiful play area.

Rebecca had thrown herself completely into redecorating one of the bedrooms for her grandson's. She had filled it with a variety of toys including a set of trains and tracks, which encircled the entire top of the room. With one click of the switch, the train whistle blew as it chugged around the top of the room. On one trip to Philadelphia, Rebecca couldn't restrain herself and bought enough clothes to fill the twin's closet. Every time the boys came to visit, she thought they grew to look more and more like Joseph.

The Devon home was now filled with hope and it was obvious to the people of Mercyville that the Devons were finally back to being the same people that they had once known.

It had been two plus months since the start of the Kohler house. Shortly after the ground breaking, Franz Kohler and Carl returned to New York City. With the rapid construction, it looked as though he would get his wish of having it completed by fall.

The two story, chalet type house had large glass windows, massive beams and a large wrap-around porch. Vaulted ceilings and large expanses of wall were purposely designed to display his extensive collections of fine art and artifacts. As an art dealer, Franz had traveled extensively and was privileged to be exposed to the finest art in the world. He planned this second home with the specific purpose of entertaining his ever-widening list of influential clients.

Everyday Martin went to Franz's property, he became more intrigued with the every growing house. Two days ago, Franz had called Martin and asked him to get rid of everything in the cabin as he was having it remodeled and refurnished. Martin again found himself in the Free Stuff business. It was really too much to carry outside so he put another large Free Stuff sign, with a large red arrow, out front, directing the interested parties to the cabin. A few minutes after putting up the sign, takers for the merchandise started arriving. People simply backed up their trucks to the porch and the excavation of the used merchandise went out of the door. After three hours, the cabin was practically empty. Martin thought this was a lot better way of getting rid of the furniture and miscellaneous items than carrying it all outside by himself. He was becoming a connoisseur of Free Stuff marketing!

At four o'clock, the last remnants of the Aarons brother' belongings had been dispensed throughout the Endless Mountains.

Just as he was getting ready to go home, a State Trooper's car pulled up in the front of the cabin. He got out and met Martin on the porch.

"Are you Martin Benson?" he asked.

"Yes I am," Martin replied.

"Then you must be the one who had the barrel table?" the officer asked.

"Yes, I had the table," Martin said with a puzzled look on his face.

"I just stopped to tell you that we are finished with the investigation of the skeletal remains and have no evidence that it was William Meredith. The dental records proved it wasn't Meredith. At this point, we just aren't sure who it is. We questioned both of the Aarons and of course they didn't admit to knowing anything about the man. The

Coroner said that both legs and the pelvis were broken. He thought that a car could have hit the man. In the bottom of the barrel, they found a gold ring engraved with initials JMB." He reached in his pocket and pulled out a small plastic bag with the ring and asked Martin if he had ever seen it before.

Martin turned white and started shaking. He became so weak, that he had to sit down on the step.

"Mr. Benson, are you all right?" the officer asked.

"That was my father's ring. He never took it off. My mother gave it to him one Christmas before she died," Martin said.

"Oh, my God!" the officer said. The Coroner is going to be shocked when he hears this. I am sorry about this whole situation, Mr. Benson. We're going to have to go back and have another talk with the Aaron brothers. I'll be back in touch with you shortly. Are you sure that you are going to be all right?" he said.

"I'll be ok," Martin half-whispered.

The last time Martin saw his father was over twelve years ago. Regardless of what the Aarons had said, he knew they had killed his father. He thought about the skull rolling out of the barrel and all he could think was that his father had come home at last. Just when he thought the barrel incident couldn't get any worse, it did. After the officer left, he just sat on the steps of the cabin for a long while. Patch had come up on the porch and lay down next to him.

It was fortunate for the Aaron brothers that they were in jail or the way Martin felt now, he would have killed both of them.

Two days later, the officer stopped out at Martin's home. He was outside chopping wood when the he approached.

"Mr. Benson, I just wanted you to know that we went back and talked to the Aarons. They finally admitted that they killed the man. Rich was driving and said it was and accident. It was raining and he said that he didn't see him. When they got out of the truck to check the man, he was already dead. They were afraid of being arrested if they called the police so they put him in the barrel in the barn. The Aarons will never again see the light of day outside of the prison walls.

I'm really sorry," the officer said.

He reached in his pocket and handed Martin the plastic bag with the gold ring in it.

"The Coroner said he would release the remains for burial. Just give him a call," he said and handed him a piece of paper with the phone number and apologized again to Martin for his misfortune.

When the officer left, he went in to the cabin and put the plastic bag with the ring in it on top of the cherry bureau, just in front of the picture of his Mother and Father.

Four days later, Martin's Father was laid to rest, next to his Mother, in the small Mercyville cemetery. The Devon Family, Matt and Alison Wallace, a few men from the conclave of opinion makers and several ladies from the Mercyville Church were there with Martin as he closed the book on the last chapter of his family.

14

Slipping into fall, the Endless Mountains took on a palette of brilliant colors. The suntanned faces of the seasonal campers became less obvious to the locals of Mercyville as most of them had returned to the concrete walls of the city. Weekends on the fall calendar of the Fairgrounds were filled with the County Fair, Trade and Sports Shows and a number of craft shows.

When you attended these events and saw baskets of apples for sale, you knew that it was time to check your antifreeze, as a white blanket of snow would be just around the corner.

Artisans of every kind filtered out of the mountains to display their wares at the Fairgrounds. Cabin fever wasn't on the agenda of the inhabitants of the surrounding mountains. It seemed as though everyone in the area was blessed with a wide range of talent to tide them over the long cold winters. The natural resources of the area were evident from the beautiful wreaths and wood products for sale. From the display of drawings and paintings being judged, it seemed that everyone was on some rung of the ladder of artistic talent. Wood sculptors, with chain saws, turned downed trees into objects of art, some of which were gigantic animals, unique benches, well designed tables and life-size figures. Even a downed tree had hope of a new beginning when it was in the hands of a chain saw sculptor.

At the Fairgrounds, after walking around, it felt good to sit down on a bench, sip a cup of cider and just watch the people as they came and went through the gates of creative adventure. Fall was the time to gather with friends in the community. Socializing became less frequent in the winter as planning activities were last minute events dictated and controlled by the weather.

For Martin Benson, fall was a busy time. Cutting enough firewood to sell to the locals and also for him took a great deal of time. With working part-time for Franz and helping Dr.Devon occasionally, his schedule was pretty full. To add to that, Charles Devon had asked him to come to West Knob and cut up some of his downed trees so he could use it in his house and also for Paul's new home. He said his caretaker, Ben Jenkins, would help him, so he thought that wouldn't be too bad.

Patch had gotten over his embarrassing surgery and evidently didn't hold it against Martin. Where Martin went, his companion was within shadow range.

Martin was coming to terms with the unfortunate death of his Father. Several times, members of the conclave had seen Martin at the cemetery putting flowers on his parent's grave.

He was beginning to have choices in respect to the direction of his life. Over the past six months, he had found unsolicited employment with Mr. Franz Kohler, worked with Dr. Devon, been asked to join the opinion makers for coffee, acquired a four legged companion, become a connoisseur of Free Stuff merchandising, and through a series of unfortunate events, been reunited with his long, lost Father. He thought back to the time when he lived behind the security of his fence and now he believed that the old Martin must have come down with the layers of warning signs.

Now that the summer mowing was over, it was taking less time working at Franz's property. He had filled the good bones barn with plenty of firewood; enough to supply both the new house and the renovated cabin for at least a year. The contractors were just about finished with the house and the interior decorator had been out several times checking on the final detail of the building extravaganza. The carpenters had removed several of the walls in the cabin and were replacing the old windows with large, double pane ones that would give the guests a panoramic view of the valley and the mountains. With the wall gone, it made the cabin appear much larger than its actual size. There really wasn't much for Martin to do until he heard from Mr.

Kohler. The last time he was at the property, he had asked him about taking care of the snow plowing during the winter. Martin said he would be glad to do it, but he would probably need a new plow. The one he had been using was used when he bought it and he didn't think it had much life left in it. He'd have to wait until Franz came back and see what kind of a plow he wanted to buy. In the mean time, tomorrow he would go over to West Knob and start on Mr. Devon's downed trees.

On the way home from Franz's he stopped in at West Knob and made arrangements with Ben Jenkins, the caretaker, as to what would be the best time for them to start cutting wood. When he saw Ben's dog, Beau, he wondered if he should bring Patch along to work with him. Ben thought it would be all right and didn't have a problem with the two canines being together. With summer behind them, Ben, like Martin, had less work to do since they were no longer mowing and keeping up the grounds. Actually, Ben was looking forward to the exercise and working with Martin. He hadn't seen Martin since the night he was at West Knob during the kidnappings over two years ago. Ben often thought if it hadn't been for Martin, the out come of the two Mercyville women might have been a lot different. It seemed to Ben that God had put the right person, at the right place, at just the right time.

The next day, as Martin drove up the long driveway to the mansion, Patch held his head out of the window allowing his ears to flap in the breeze.

Ben was out front as he pulled up. Patch spotted Beau and for the first time, he jumped out of the truck window and headed toward Beau. Both dogs stood their ground and did the customary sniffing ritual of each other. Patch knew this was Beau's territory and instinctively backed away from him. As the two men started talking, the two dogs raced around the grounds as if they were old friends. Beau knew his perimeters and Patch knew he was a guest within that circle.

While the men worked on the trees, the dogs explored the nearby woods. They attempted to chase a few rabbits and squirrels but, Beau was too old to run fast and Patch was too young to be smart enough for the catch.

After several hours of sawing and stacking, Ben and Martin decided that it was time for a break. Ben went in to his apartment, above the carriage house, and returned with two cold colas. Martin suddenly realized that he was starting to enjoy the carbonated beverage and may invest in a six pack to keep in his springhouse.

As the two men were resting, Beau and Patch came running up on the porch. Each was carrying a leg bone of a deer. When Ben took a closer look, he realized that someone had killed the white deer.

Dr. Devon was not going to be at all happy about this. Paul had a special rapport with the white deer and considered the young buck to be a sign of good fortune. Whoever killed the white deer, was walking under the curse of misfortune. The spirit of the white deer seemed to come alive through Paul.

Ben and Martin followed the dogs in to the woods and found the scattered remains of the white buck. The deer lived and died at West Knob but his spirit had spread over the mountain and that could never be touched. The ghost of the white deer would remain over West Knob for all eternity and woe be the person who had shaken the wrath of the mighty young buck.

When Paul found out about the death of the white deer, he went in to the forest, gathered up his bones and buried them near the Devon family cemetery. Paul would never again speak of the white deer and when he buried him, he buried his spirit deep within his heart.

Martin and Ben had spent the last five days cutting, stacking and moving the wood for the Devons' fireplaces and felt they had harvested enough to last through the winter. Both men were tired and glad that the job was finished.

As Martin and Patch headed home, he decided to treat himself to a pack of cola. As he pulled in to the country store/post office, unfamiliar vehicles were crowded in the parking lot. When he went in to the store, he could see that the table of the opinion makers had been taken over by outsiders with clipboards, stacks of miscellaneous papers, headsets wrapped around their necks, cell phones and a tall women who seemed to be the ringleader of the group.

"Martin asked the store clerk what was going on?"

'She said the group was from a TV station in Philadelphia and they were traveling around the state making a documentary film on old homes. Evidently, she said, they had picked several homes in the area to feature in the film. They said they had contacted the Devons for West Knob, Mary Ellen Weatherstone for her Bed and Breakfast and Molly Anderson for her Victorian house and antique shop. What they didn't have was an original old cabin to represent the first homesteaders in the area and that they had been inquiring of the locals if anyone knew where they could find a cabin. Matt Wallace suggested you might be interested in having them take a look at your cabin?'

"I don't know about that!" Martin said. "It's just an old cabin that my great-grandfather built. Who would want a picture of that?"

Just then the ring leader of the TV crew walked up to the store clerk and asked her if she knew where she could find a Martin Benson? The clerk looked at Martin and said, "This is Mr. Benson standing right next to you."

Well, this was easy enough she thought, as she introduced herself to Martin. She explained the mission, in detail, which really didn't seem to impress him one iota. All he came in the store for was a six pack of cola and now some outsider wanted to put he and his cabin on television. Things in Mercyville were moving a little to fast for him. He needed time to roll everything over in his mind.

"Now, what do you think of that idea, Mr. Benson? Can we use your cabin in our show?" the ringleader asked.

"I'm going to have to think about it. You can get a hold of me tomorrow. I'm on my way home. I've had a busy day," Martin said, as he walked out of the store with his pack of cola.

The ringleader was taken back with his attitude. Why, she thought, everyone wants to be on TV. This guy wasn't going to be too easy to work with, but she didn't have a choice. She needed a cabin and he seemed to be the only one with an original homestead in the area.

"Get those lights tilted a little more to the right," the ringleader of the TV crew directed.

Charles Devon was seated in front of the make-up artist's mirror while she painted his face with several layers of paste and powders. He was intrigued with the notion of having West Knob featured in a documentary. The night before he stood in front of the bedroom mirror practicing his one paragraph synopsis about his historic home. This was totally out of character for the dignified owner of the mansion. Rebecca joined in the fun and was making a home video of her own of the chaos playing out in her living room. Ben Jenkins, the caretaker, just stood in the background watching the whole chaotic fiasco. It took two hours of preparation to get everything in order. As the camera started to roll, Charles Devon and the historical mansion made their first television debut. No sooner than Charles had gotten warmed up, the ringleader yelled "that's a wrap". With what seemed to the Devons to be super human speed, the equipment was dismantled, packed up and the crew was out of the front door and on their way to Mary Ellen Weatherstone's Bed and Breakfast. All Charles Devon was left with was a skin irritation from all of the make-up and the satisfaction that he had made his first and most likely his last TV appearance.

Mary Ellen had spent several days preparing her home for the television crew. She also spent hours writing a four-page dissertation of the house, the original builders, and the history of the previous owners. To her dismay, the ringleader cut her speech to three lines and no sooner had they arrived, they were out of the door and on their way to Molly Anderson's Victorian two story house with the Antique shop.

Molly, like the Devons and the Weatherstone's, experienced the crash entrance and a swift exit. It was so fast, she wondered if she had just dreamt the whole experience.

Definite permission had yet to be given by Martin to the TV crew to film his cabin. As they pulled up in front of Martin's fence, the head of the crew got out of the truck and walked up to the reposed man in his lawn chair drinking one of his colas.

"Mr. Benson, we were wondering if you had decided to let us film your cabin?" the boss lady asked.

"Well," Martin said, "I was thinking about it! Maybe you can come back tomorrow morning and do it, but you have to have Patch in the picture. He's my only family now, so he has to be there too. I decided that I'm just going to say one line about the cabin and that's all!"

The ringleader, boss lady, still didn't like Martin's attitude but she was stuck to find another cabin. Reluctantly, she agreed to his terms and said they would be back in the morning.

That evening, Martin prepared himself for his morning debut. He trimmed his hair and organized his wardrobe for the morning shoot. He gave Patch a quickie bath and a good brushing. Over and over again he kept saying his one line. "My great-grandfather built this cabin and now it belongs to me." After hours of using Patch as a sounding board, Martin thought he had it down pat. Now all he needed was a good night's sleep.

At ten-thirty in the morning, the TV crew rolled up in front of Martin's homestead. Both Martin, who was neatly attired, and Patch, who was wearing a red, white and blue patriotic scarf around his neck, were out front looking spit and polished as the whole crew descended upon his property. Lights went up, cameras were put in place and it seemed to Martin that everyone was screaming directions to each other. After forty-five minutes of organization, the ringleader, boss lady, placed Martin in front of his cabin with Patch by his side. After a much back and forth heated discussion about taking the dog out of the picture, the 'let him in side' finally won out.

As the camera zoomed in for a close-up of Martin's face, the ringleader hadn't noticed that Patch had gotten up, walked up next to her and relieved himself all over her foot!

Whether or not he understood the debate over his premiere TV appearance, we will never know, but regardless, the once stray dog wasn't going to be treated lightly and ended up having the last word.

Those involved in the recent documentary of historic homes, by the Philadelphia television station, were slowly recovering from their fifteen minutes of fame experience. As for Martin Benson, he never again wanted to see any more TV people. Of course the ringleader of the TV crew wasn't interested in going back to Martin's cabin after Patch relieved himself on her new, high-priced, Amanda Dandee brand shoes!

Charles Devon laid out one hundred and twenty five dollars to an Edwardton dermatologist for an exam and anti-biotic to get rid of the skin rash he developed which was brought on by the layers of make-up applied to his face for his TV debut.

With the quick entrance and exit of the TV crew, Mary Ellen Weatherstone and Molly Anderson still weren't sure the event actually took place or if it was just a figment of their imaginations. The only way they would be convinced that it happened would be when they saw it on TV.

Everything in Mercyville seemed to be back to normal. No longer could the village be called Plain Jane after the mounting events of the past two years. The kidnappings, the now explained unfortunate killing of Martin Benson's father, the arrest of the Aaron brothers and now with the television documentary, it seemed as though the village was receiving its share of publicity. Now, all they needed was a large discount store and it would revel any other town of the same size.

Down at the country store/post office, the only concern the conclave of opinion makers had was what happened to William Meredith, the Edwardton hunter, who had disappeared. The old newspapers had said he was last seen in the Mercyville area during deer hunting season two years ago. Martin was the closest to finding any clue as to his whereabouts when he found the wallet, hunting license and the newspaper articles. The police had searched the old Aaron property thoroughly but hadn't come up with a body or any other clues. Meredith's paper work was sealed in a manila envelope in a metal cabinet at the Sheriff's office and filed under Cold Cases.

The opinion makers prided themselves on solving the problems of the world and the surrounding country over coffee every morning but the Meredith case had them stumped.

15

Dr. Devon had been thinking about putting up a small barn behind his clinic for large animal treatment. He thought if he could get Martin to help him, they could get it done a lot faster than waiting for a contractor. He had drawn up a one-story barn with five stalls and a storage area for hay and feed. That way, the farmers and those with large animals could bring them to the clinic where Paul would be able to treat them and he could keep them there for as long as they needed treatment.

It was October and if they worked fast, they could build the barn in four weeks. Paul drove over to Franz Kohler's house to see if Martin was there. As he pulled in the driveway, Patch came running up to the truck, so he knew Martin must be close by. As he got out of the truck, Martin came out of the barn and up to meet him.

"How's it going, Martin?" Paul asked.

"Pretty good, Dr. Devon," Martin said.

"Why I stopped, Martin was to ask you if you would help me with a building project? I brought along the plans," he said.

Martin looked at the plans and they didn't look too complicated to him.

"I think we can get it done before the snow flies," Martin said.

"I was hoping you would say that," Paul said. "I'll order the materials from Edwardton Building Supply Company today and see how soon they can get them here. I found a local man who has a bulldozer who said he would level the area as soon as I decided when I wanted to start. I'll give him a call as soon as I get back to the clinic.

He said he would put in the footers too. I'll keep in touch and let you know when we can start the building. Thanks again, Martin."

"Looking at Patch," he said. "That's a good companion you have there. I just can't picture you without Patch." He got back in his truck and headed back to the clinic.

Four days later, the ground had been leveled behind the clinic and the footers had been put in. Now Paul and Martin could start on the building.

The framing of the barn went fast. An electrician was scheduled to come in a few days to get the electrical done. In a week all of the sides were done and the roof in place. Once the roof was covered they didn't have to worry about the weather and could begin work on the stalls. It was a simple job, as the front of the stalls would have metal swing gates. Sliding metal doors were placed at each end of the barn, allowing a truck to be driven through. Periodically Martin would have to stop for a few hours and help Dr. Devon on a large animal call. Martin had been doing this on a regular basis and enjoyed the work. When he went on a call with Paul, he put Patch in one of the kennels until they got back.

The clinic was like a second home to Patch and he enjoyed being outside with Martin as he was working.

The ground had been packed down so that sawdust or straw could be used for bedding. For feeding, corner mangers had been placed in each stall.

As Martin was putting up the first gate on the end stall, Patch was at the other end of the barn sniffing and digging at the packed ground. Dr. Devon walked in and witnessed the furious pace at which the canine was digging up the dirt-packed barn floor. He went closer to the excavation site to get a better look at what Patch was so intent on digging. He looked in the hole and at first he thought it was a deer bone but after brushing some of the dirt away, he realized he was looking at part of a human jawbone. By this time Martin had finished with the stall gate and was walking toward Paul and Patch. He thought of Martin's past experience with the barrel and skull and stopped him from coming any closer.

“Martin, I don’t think you want to go over there,” Paul said.

Martin was puzzled and asked what was wrong? When he saw the hole, his first thought was that Paul was mad about Patch digging the hole but by the look on his face, he knew it was more serious.

“Let’s go in to the clinic and bring Patch along with you,” he said.

When they were inside, Paul tried gently to explain to Martin what Patch had dug up. He didn’t think Martin needed another visual stuck in his mind of a skull and have it bring back all of the old memories.

Martin took what Paul had explained a lot better than expected. He said he would have to call the Sheriff and get them out to the clinic.

While waiting for the Sheriff, Martin went to the refrigerator and got a cola. He and Patch waited there until the Sheriff arrived. Martin didn’t say much but Paul knew the past had crept back in to his mind. He felt bad that Martin was there when he found the jawbone, but if it weren’t for Patch, no one would ever have known it was there.

The front door of the clinic opened and closed with the sound of sleigh bells on the front door. Paul greeted the Sheriff and his officer as they walked in to the clinic. He explained what Patch had dug up and led them out the back door to the newly built barn. The Sheriff studied the partially buried jawbone and had his officer surround the barn with the yellow crime scene tape. He called the crime scene unit and the Coroner to come out to the clinic.

“I’m not really sure what to make of this,” the Sheriff said. “We’ll have dig up the stall and see what else is there. It’s a good thing the Martin’s dog dug this up or we would never have known it was here.”

Within a half-hour the new barn was filled with officials who were taking pictures and slowly digging around the exposed jawbone. Martin stood in the background with a somber look on his face. Dr. Devon put Patch in one of the kennels to keep him out of the way of the ongoing excavation. As the Crime unit slowly removed the dirt, more skeletal remains began to appear.

Paul had called his father to come down to the clinic. When he arrived, he walked through the clinic and out the back door to the barn. He joined his son and Martin who were watching the dig.

“What the Devil is going on here?” Charles Devon asked.

"Patch was digging in the end stall as Martin was putting a gate on the stall at the opposite end of the barn. I looked to see what he was digging and the rest is history," Paul replied.

"Does anyone have any idea who it is?" Charles asked.

"Not at this point. We'll just have to wait until the Coroner examines the remains. The whole thing is a mystery. I was shocked when I realized it was human remains. I don't know what Martin must be thinking, but I'm sure old memories have flooded back in to his mind."

"Martin," Dr. Devon said, "I think we can call it a day as far as working on the barn. With all of the commotion, I almost forgot that I have something for you."

Martin and Paul walked back in to the clinic. Paul picked up a small package from his desk, opened it and handed the contents to Martin.

"I bought this cell phone for you. Since you don't have a phone at home, I thought you could use this. This way I can get a hold of you if I have an emergency call and I need you to assist," Paul said.

"You're going to have to show me how this thing works," he said, with a puzzled look on his face.

Dr. Devon gave him a quick lesson in the use of the cell phone and how it operated. When that was finished, Martin then became a full-fledged member of the twenty-first century.

"One other thing Martin," he said, as he opened the clinic's closet. He reached inside, pulled out a white jacket and handed it to Martin. I thought since you were my assistant you needed this. On the pocket of the jacket, stitched in blue letters, it said: "Martin, Veterinarian Assistant".

He was surprised at both of the gifts. He didn't think the work he did for Dr. Devon was important enough to have his own jacket but since he bought it for him, he would wear it whenever he worked at the clinic.

For a few moments, he had forgotten about what was happening in the newly constructed barn. He took the gifts, went to the kennel, got Patch and called it a day. His mind was slipping back to thoughts of his Father, which drifted in and out of his mind.

After Martin left for home, Paul went back out to the barn. The members of the crime unit had uncovered a complete skull and were working their way down the torso and arms. From what had been revealed so far, it appeared that the remains were clothed. The color of the remaining hair was difficult to determine with the amount of dirt on it. Paul could see what appeared to be gold backing on the front teeth. He asked the Sheriff how long he thought it would take to remove the remains? He estimated several more hours and then the barn could be released back to Paul.

Paul's father, Charles, was watching intently as members of the Crime Unit continue to dig. As Paul walked up next to him, his father asked again if he had any idea as to who it might be?

"I don't have a clue. To the best of my knowledge, no one from Mercyville had been reported missing. The only person that I know about that is missing is that hunter from Edwarton. From what Martin had said, from the old newspaper article he found at Franz's, Meredith had been hunting around Mercyville. The whole thing is very strange, especially the remains showing up on our property. It really gives me chills to think about it. If it weren't for Patch digging up the bones, no one would have ever known the remains were here," Paul said.

It was starting to get dark when the Crime Unit had finished with the dig. They had recovered the remains of what appeared to be a complete skeleton. They were bagged and put in to the Coroner's van.

Word had spread around Mercyville that the police were at Paul Devon's clinic. All afternoon people reduced their speed as they drove by and began to rubberneck hoping to get a glance at what was unfolding at the clinic. Since the crime scene was out back behind the clinic building, very little could be seen as to what was actually happening.

The Sheriff told Paul they were finished with the excavation and turned the barn back over to him. The nine by nine-foot stall had been completely dug up and would have to be leveled and packed down again.

Paul wondered if the death of the white deer made him shed his wrath upon the mountain. Was this the end of some terrible event or was it the beginning of something even more sinister to come. Only time would tell.

It was eight-thirty Tuesday morning and the conclave of opinion makers were seated around the large round table at the country store. The new coffee machine was getting plenty of use as it belched out a variety of caffeinated beverages. The buzz among the opinion makers was what had happened out at Paul Devon's Vet Clinic the day before. Only bits and pieces of information had filtered out through Mercyville. Each time someone talked about the happening, it was prefixed by 'I'm not sure about this but...or Don't take my word for it but...!'

It was obvious that no one had the complete story except Martin and Dr. Devon. Of course if you wanted it direct from the horse's mouth, Patch, if he could talk, would have been the best and most credible source.

As the buzz continued around the table, Martin Benson walked in to the store to get a replacement for his six pack of cola. He was on his way to the clinic and was wearing the white jacket that Paul had given him. Matt Wallace called Martin over to the table and asked him to join them for coffee. He also asked him if he knew anything about what had happened at the clinic?

Martin passed on the coffee but did volunteer information on what actually happened at the new barn. He figured the truth was better than a lot of hearsay floating around the village. The men at the table were spellbound as Martin gave an accurate account as to what had taken place the day before. Just as he was about finished talking, the ring of his cell phone interrupted him. It was Dr. Devon and he wanted Martin to pick up several bales of hay before he came to the clinic.

"I have to be on my way," Martin said. "Dr. Devon needs some hay to be picked up."

After Martin had left, the chatter continued around the table. The opinion makers couldn't believe it was the same Martin Benson. He had really changed over the past two years. He had definitely found his place among the town folk of Mercyville.

As he drove up to the clinic, he could see that Dr. Devon was having trouble getting a horse out of a horse trailer. The equine didn't want to get out so Martin got in one side to the two-horse trailer and gently pushed the horse backwards. After a couple of tries and some soft-spoken words, the horse backed out. Dr. Devon grabbed the lead rope and took the horse to the barn. It had a cut on its leg and he would have to stitch it.

It was a lot easier having Martin there to help, thought Paul. It seemed to him that Martin was a natural working around animals. He was never in a hurry and let an animal take its time until it felt at ease.

After getting the horse settled, Martin went back to putting up the gates in the on the other stalls. He had no sooner started than Dr. Devon came out to the barn.

"Martin, you'll have to stop what you're doing and come with me. I have an emergency call out on Branch Creek Road. Something is wrong with two horses out there," he said.

Martin put on his white jacket, got in the truck and they headed out. When they arrived at the pasture, where the two horses were, they couldn't believe what they saw. The horses were staggering around as though they were inebriated. The owner said the horses had gotten out of the fence during the night and when they found them they were in the apple orchard and were weaving around as they walked!

It didn't take Paul long to figure out what was wrong. The horses were drunk! They had gotten into the apple orchard and had gotten some bad apples. There wasn't much he could do now. Eventually, it would wear off. He told the owner to just keep an eye on them and make sure they didn't get out again!

Martin had never seen anything like that before and Dr. Devon said he had heard about animals getting drunk on bad apples, but had never seen it before today. It was a strange and wonderful world of animals into which Martin now found himself.

Driving to the clinic he asked Paul what he thought about finding the remains in the barn?

"I don't know what to think, Martin. It could be that missing Meredith man. Then I wondered why the two licenses and the newspaper articles were at the Aarons' place. It seems awfully suspicious. Why would they keep those newspaper articles? There are just too many unanswered questions. I guess we'll just have to wait and see what the police come up with," Paul said.

"I have a feeling the Aarons had something to do with the whole thing. They're just no good. After kidnapping you and the women and then killing my father, I feel like I could kill them if I got a hold of them," Martin said.

This was the first time Martin had ever talked to Paul about the past and the Aarons.

"I know everything they've done is tragic but they'll never get of prison. Try not to think about it. It's all out of our hands now. We'll just have to wait and see what the police come up with," Paul replied.

Back at the clinic, Martin continued putting gates on the stalls in the barn. When he finished he would begin filling in the excavated stall.

Suzanne Devon, Paul's wife, had brought lunch down to the clinic. She was expecting her first child in two months and everyone was hoping that it would be Christmas baby.

As she started out to the barn, Paul and Martin were just coming inside.

"I think it's time for you two men to take a break. I brought lunch since I knew neither one of you would stop to eat," Suzanne said.

The three were sitting in Paul's office eating and Patch was there begging for a handout.

The repast was interrupted by the sound of sleigh bells as the clinic door opened. A clink, clink, clink came from the bell on the counter in the waiting room.

Paul got up and went to answer the call. It was Miss Doris, Franz Kohler's neighbor, with her white pregnant poodle.

"I think that Precious Babe is having labor pains. She just keeps pacing back and forth and she won't eat," Miss Doris said.

" Bring her back and I'll examine her," Paul told her.

When Miss Doris and her poodle passed Paul's office, make shift lunchroom, Martin saw who it was and slid down in his chair so she wouldn't recognize him. It was his beloved Patch who caused

Precious Babe to become pregnant. When Patch saw Miss Doris and the pregnant poodle, he slid under Dr. Devon's desk as though he remembered he was the culprit!

"Just put Precious on the table," Paul said.

After a minute or so, he announced that the poodle was in labor and would have her pups shortly.

"Leave Precious here and I'll call you as soon as she delivers. I don't think it will be long now," he said.

Miss Doris left the office as the doctor settled the poodle in to a whelping box.

As her returned to his office to finish his lunch, he congratulated Martin and Patch on their soon to be extended family! Martin was just embarrassed for Patch who could have cared less. After all, it was Precious Babe who caused him to lose his reproductive anatomy!

An hour and a half later, Precious had delivered seven beautiful and healthy pups; four of which were carbon copies of Patch. Martin couldn't deny that the pups were definitely Patch's.

The clink, clink, clink of the desk bell rang again. Paul walked out and was greeted by the Sheriff.

"I just came by to let you know that those remains from your barn have been positively identified as William Meredith from Edwardton. His wife had supplied his dental records when he was first reported missing. There's no question about it. It is Meredith and he died from a gunshot wound to the head. The Aaron brother's are going to have a lot of explaining to do. We're going over to the prison tomorrow to talk to them. We want to know how they got his wallet and hunting license. At this point, it doesn't look good for them," the Sheriff said.

"Thank you for stopping by. At least we know who it is and there won't be any more speculation. I'd appreciate knowing what the Aarons have to say," Paul said.

After we talk to them, I'll be in touch with you." the Sheriff said as he left the office.

Suzanne had left the clinic and gone home. Martin was back out in the barn trying to replace the dirt in the excavated stall. Paul went out to the barn and told Martin what the Sheriff had disclosed.

"Them Aarons are just plain no good," Martin said. "As long as they've been in Mercyville, they've always caused some kind of trouble. Even behind bars they're still causing trouble."

"We'll just have to wait and see what the Sheriff finds out tomorrow," Dr.Devon said.

The barn was completed at the Devon clinic and Martin would have some time off from his work with the doctor. If he was needed at the clinic, Paul would contact him by way of his cell phone. With the money that Paul had paid him for building the barn, he decided to go to Edwardton and make a deposit in his first ever savings account. He thought it felt good knowing he had a little money in the bank. While he was in Edwardton he would splurge and buy himself a few groceries plus a box of dog biscuits for Patch.

When he walked in the Save-Big Super Market, they had a special sale on beef and chicken so he got several packages of each. Down at the end of the meat case, there was a Free sign with bags of large bones so he took a bag for Patch. Martin didn't care too much for pastries but the cherry pie that Mrs. Devon had sent over to him during the barrel skull incident tasted good. He picked up a pie and added it to his cart then filled up the remaining space with can goods, dry products and a gallon of milk. As he was headed for the checkout line, he noticed a display of cola; his favorite carbonated beverage and put a six pack in his cart.

As he was standing in line, he noticed that the lady in front of him was writing a check for her groceries. The names on the check were William and Betty Meredith. He wanted to ask her if it was her husband who had been the missing hunter in Mercyville but what if she hadn't heard yet that he had been found? Martin thought it was better if he didn't say anything. He didn't want to be the one to break the news, especially at the Big-Save Super Market. If it was Meredith's wife, she had been through enough in the past two years.

Driving through Edwardton, toward home, he spotted the dollar store, He had never been in there before so he thought he would stop. When he went inside of the store, he was amazed at all the things you could buy for a dollar. He picked up several bowls, a couple of blue glasses and some thick white candles. In the craft section, among the array of paints and brushes, he spotted some wood carving tools. He liked woodcarving but he hadn't carved since he was a teenager. It might be interesting to try carving again so he put a variety of tools in his basket. Just as he was about to leave, he spotted a shelf with dog bowls and he picked one up for Patch. It was white with black paw prints around the sides. At this point, he thought he had better checkout, as the dollar store held too many temptations for him!

Driving back from Edwardton, a few snowflakes were coming down. Patch, sitting on the front seat with his head out of the window, didn't seem mind as the flakes started piling up on his head!

When he pulled in to his private drive, the first light snow of the season had sprinkled across the ground. Martin unloaded the purchases he had gotten in Edwardton and stacked everything neatly on the shelves. He put some dog food in Patch's dish and shortly the dog had christened his new dinnerware.

Martin stoked the fire in the stove and put on another log. The cabin wasn't very large but it was cozy and was sufficient for both man and beast. Tomorrow he would go over to Franz Kohler's place and check on how the building was coming along. He hoped with the snow on the way that Franz would get back to Mercyville soon and let him know about getting a new snowplow.

16

When Martin pulled in at Franz's house, he could see that the carpenters were still there. He got out of the truck and went in to the latest extravaganza in Mercyville. Patch took off when he spotted a rabbit sitting near the front of the wrap-around deck.

"Good morning, Martin," the carpenter said. "We'll be finishing up here shortly. We just have a little more molding to put up and that should be it. Oh, yes, Mr. Kohler called and said he would be here Saturday." As he reached in his pocket, he pulled out a key and handed it to Martin. "He said to give you the key since we wouldn't be coming back anymore."

Martin took the key and put it on the key ring next to the one from the cabin.

"Did Mr. Kohler say he wanted me to get any supplies for the house and the cabin?"

"He didn't say but I assume that he'll have a list of what he needs when he gets here," the carpenter said.

"I thought now that everyone is finished working in the house, I would start bringing in the firewood and stacking some out on the deck," Martin said.

"Oh, yes, I almost forgot. Mr. Kohler did say the Interior Decorator was planning on having all of the furniture delivered this Thursday and he was wondering if you could be here to oversee the delivery. I guess by the way he talked, it's quite a lot of furniture. It's for the house and the cabin. He said they should be here around nine o'clock," the carpenter said.

"I'll be here at eight-thirty just in case they get here early. I'm going over to the cabin and see how close they are to finishing. I want to make sure everything is done before the furniture arrives," Martin said.

He walked over to the cabin and went inside. It didn't even look like the old cabin. With the walls removed, the living room was huge and the new windows now allowed for a panoramic view of the mountains and valley. The old kitchen was totally replaced and the size increased by twenty feet. Five, huge, cherry wood support columns replaced the walls that had been removed. The large dormer bedroom had been made into two large bedrooms with a center hall bath. Standing on the balcony of the loft, you could see the open living room and the kitchen area. Two beautiful reproduction Tiffany lamps had been placed in the dining area and the kitchen.

The only person in the cabin was the electrician who had just finished hanging the lamps.

"The carpenter left an envelope on the kitchen counter. They found it behind one of the old kitchen cabinets," the electrician said, and he packed up his equipment and headed out the front door as Patch was running up the steps of the porch. He sniffed around the cabin, as practically everything there was new to him.

He walked over to the kitchen counter and picked up the manila envelope. He would put it in his truck and give it to Franz on Saturday.

There was no electricity at Martin's homestead, but now that he had money in the bank and after looking at the reproduction Tiffany lamps, he decided that he might start to modernize.

The electrician was still putting his equipment in his truck as Martin locked up the cabin and walked down the steps.

"You wouldn't have time to come out to my cabin, would you?" he asked the electrician. "I was thinking about putting electricity in, well, that is if it doesn't cost too much."

"Sure, Martin, I can stop by tomorrow afternoon. I have a job to do tomorrow morning in Edwardton and I can stop on my way home," he said.

With that arranged, Martin and his sidekick headed home.

After a quick lunch and his daily cola, he started cutting and stacking more wood. To him, the sky looked like snow and he wanted to make sure that he had plenty of wood for the stove. He had a small carport type structure behind his cabin where he parked his truck in the winter and at one end of it he had stacked several cords of wood. He was ready for winter.

The next afternoon the electrician stopped by and gave Martin an estimate of how much it would cost to electrify his cabin. He didn't realize how small his cabin was and knew it wouldn't take long to get the job done.

Martin agreed to the estimate and arranged a time for the work to be done. With a handshake, a new cell phone and now with electricity on the way, Martin was headed full speed in to a world called modern!

It was eight-thirty Thursday morning when he arrived at Franz Kohler's house. On the way over he stopped by the clinic and put Patch in one of the kennels. He didn't want him in the way of the furniture deliverymen and anyway Dr. Devon liked having Patch at the clinic.

At eight-fifty, the Interior Decorator from Edwardton drove in the driveway in her new red Jaguar. Martin thought decorating Franz's house must have really paid off.

She walked over to Martin and started giving instructions as to what should go where when the furniture arrived.

"I'll take care of the house and the furniture placement. I would like you handle the cabin. Make sure the men don't hit the walls when they come in and make sure they put down plastic runners so they don't mark up the floors and rugs," she barked.

As she continued giving orders, Martin blanked the commands out of his mind. After all, there are just so many orders a man can take at one time. She was still babbling when two large furniture trucks pulled in to the driveway. She walked over to the drivers and started giving orders and pointing in the direction of the house and cabin with her cashmere-covered arms.

At least she would be in the house and out of his hair, thought Martin. The house is her territory and the cabin is mine. He was really glad he had left Patch at the clinic because this woman would have gone into a total panic if the poor dog had walked on the new floors.

Martin asked the delivery truck with the cabin furniture to back up to the porch. As he looked across the lawn to the newly built house. Dolly Decorator was in front of the truck waving directions as how close to get to the wrap-around porch. He felt sorry for the men with the house furniture. No matter what they did today, it wasn't going to suit the cashmere princess. As the men brought the furniture in to the cabin, Martin made himself useful by taking off the rolls of bubble wrap around most of the pieces. As the furniture was uncovered, he thought even though Dolly Decorator was bossy, at least she seemed to have good taste. For the country style living room there were two cranberry plaid sofas with four complimentary green wingback chairs. Four end tables, four brass lamps and two large glass-top coffee tables completed the living room decor. A large cherry plank wood table with eight-ladder back chairs fit perfectly in the newly extended dining area.

Martin wasn't a decorator, but he thought a few paintings would look nice on the walls. The only piece of furniture in the cabin that wasn't given away during the Free Stuff merchandising campaign was the massive bookcase. Franz had a refinisher rejuvenate the piece and it fit in well with the new furnishings.

With the downstairs furniture in place, the men started taking the bedroom sets up to the loft. Even though it was cold outside, the poor men were perspiring. Martin went out to his truck and brought in a twelve pack of cola and offered it to the men. They didn't need their arms twisted to take him up on the offer and take a well-deserved break.

Over at the house Dolly Decorator was standing in the middle of the massive living room signaling with her arms in which direction she desired the pieces to go. All she needed was a whistle and a reflective iridescent orange vest and she could have been mistaken for a traffic officer.

After three hours, the furniture was in place, the beds were set up and the bubble wrap and boxes put back in to the truck for later disposal. The men from the cabin had finished sooner than those at the house so they went over to help them complete the unpacking. It didn't take long and the house was completely furnished. One of the men walked over to the exhausted decorator and had her sign for the two deliveries. With all of the waving and directing, her neatly combed upswept hair was now hanging in strands over her face.

The deliverymen were glad that the day was over. As they drove out the driveway, they gave Martin a thumbs-up sign and wished him well. Martin thought his day was over but just as the furniture trucks were leaving a large truck marked decorator's warehouse pulled up. They had two separate orders to be delivered. One order was for the cabin and the other was for the house. He told the men to take everything in and put it in the living room. He would look at the contents later. After they finished, he directed them over to the house. At the house, the decorator showed them where to put the boxes. After they were finished, she told Martin she would be back in the morning to open the boxes and put everything away. When the decorator warehouse truck left, the red Jaguar followed it with a disheveled and exhausted decorator.

Martin had enough excitement for one day and he headed to the clinic to pick up his dog. All wanted to do was go home and relax with Patch.

The cell phone rang and it was Dr. Devon. He asked Martin if he could come in the next afternoon. He had a horse and a cow coming in the afternoon plus a full schedule of cats and dogs coming in to be treated. Suzanne was coming in the afternoon and would take care of the front desk. Martin agreed and said he would be there at twelve-thirty. That meant the he would have a full day tomorrow.

It was Friday morning and Martin was up early. He fed Patch, straightened up the cabin and headed out to Franz's house. He stopped by the clinic again and put Patch in a kennel until he was finished unpacking. If the decorator was not going to be there he would have brought Patch along. He didn't need to get in a hassle with her over the dog. All he needed to do was get done and get over to the clinic.

He went to the cabin and started unpacking the boxes. It seemed to him that the decorator had purchased everything a home needed and more! There were stacks towels, sheets, sets of dishes, pots and pans, knick-knacks, sets of flatware, trash cans, brooms and a vacuum cleaner. He wondered what all of this cost Franz and he hoped that he had enough money left for a snowplow.

Just as he was leaving, the decorator pulled up and apologized for over sleeping. She thanked Martin for unpacking and putting away the new array of household items for the cabin. She said she would spend the afternoon unpacking everything in the house and when she left she would leave the key to the house under the terra cotta pot on the deck.

Martin wasn't a connoisseur of decorating but in his humble opinion, he thought the cabin looked pretty nice.

It was twelve-thirty when Martin arrived at the clinic. Suzanne was behind the reception counter and Paul was just finishing his lunch.

"Good afternoon, Martin," Suzanne said. "We're really glad you could work this afternoon. It seems like everyone decided to bring his animal in today. I thought you would be happy to know that Miss Doris is bringing Precious Babe and the pups in for a check up at two o'clock. I know you don't want to miss that!"

"Let me know when she gets here so I make sure I'm out in the barn!" he said.

He walked back to the closet, got out his white jacket with his name stitched in blue and put it on. He went outside and helped Dr. Devon unload a horse and put it in the barn. No sooner had the horse been settled in, a farmer pulled up with a cow. Martin directed him out back to the barn. There they unloaded the cow and put her in a stall opposite the horse.

Two dog owners and one cat owner were in the waiting room. Suzanne directed the one dog owner to examining room one and the owner of the to room number two. There was a steady pace of dogs and cats all afternoon. At four o'clock Paul and Suzanne took a much-needed break. They were sitting in Paul's office when there sounded a clink, clink, clink coming from the counter call bell. Suzanne went to the front desk to see who was there.

"May I help you?" Suzanne asked.

"Yes, the lady said in a soft-spoken voice. "I was wondering if I could talk to Dr. Devon? My name is Betty Meredith."

Suzanne went back to get Paul. He had her bring Mrs. Meredith back to his office.

Betty Meredith introduced herself and started to explain why she was there.

"My husband was William Meredith, the missing hunter from Edwardton. The Sheriff called me Wednesday and informed me that the body of my husband had been found here. I guess it's a strange request, but it would help me to put some closure to this part of my life." Betty Meredith said.

"I'm very sorry about your husband, Mrs. Meredith. We were shocked by the discovery. If we wouldn't have built the barn, I don't think he would have ever been found. I'll take you out to the barn," Paul said.

He got up and led her out to he barn. Martin was there putting out hay for the two barn patients.

"Martin, I'd like you to meet Mrs. William Meredith. William Meredith was her husband. Mrs. Meredith, this is my assistant, Martin Benson," he said.

For a few seconds, Martin was stunned and at a loss for words. It was the same woman that he had seen several days ago the Big-Save Super Market in Edwardton.

Betty Meredith was a petite lady about thirty years old. She was rather plain looking with short brown hair and a pleasant smile.

Paul took her gently by the arm and walked her over to the stall where her husband's remains were found. Tears filled her eyes as she remembered the last time she had seen him. She turned and walked to the end of the barn where Martin was standing.

"It seems rather ironic that Bill was found at a veterinary clinic. I worked at the Edwardton Animal Clinic for ten years. The owners retired last year and closed the clinic. I loved the work and being around animals. The job helped to keep me sane after Bill's disappearance. Since the Sheriff called about finding him, I feel I have had a great weight taken off of me. At least I know I can finally put him to rest. Do you have any idea how he died?" she asked.

"No, I don't know. I know that the Sheriff is looking into the case and when he comes up with something, I'm sure he'll let you know," Paul said.

He didn't want to bring up their suspicions about the Aarons because he didn't know if the Sheriff had mentioned it to her.

As they walked back in to the clinic, Paul thought he would ask her if she would be interested in working for him?

"Mrs. Meredith, as you see, my wife, Suzanne is pregnant and is due in December. She helps out here when things get busy but she can't work too much longer in her condition. I was wondering if you would be interested in working for me? We could start out part-time and as my business increases, I could put you on full-time," he said.

"I would enjoy that, Dr. Devon. I have been looking for a part-time job but haven't found anything as interesting as the work I had at the animal clinic. When you think you are ready to hire, please give me a call," Betty Meredith said.

She wrote her name and number on a piece of paper and handed it to Dr. Devon. "I'm at home almost everyday. If I'm not there, I'm only gone for a short time," she said.

She thanked him for his help and walked out of the office.

For Mrs. Meredith, closure had finally come and another door was about to open.

The Sheriff walked in to the Delville Prison and asked to talk with Tom and Rich Aaron. The outside door buzzed and when he opened it a guard escorted him to a small room with a table and two chairs. In a few minutes, the guard brought the handcuffed Rich Aaron in to the room. He was dressed in an orange jumpsuit and didn't look pleased to see the Sheriff. He sat down and wondered what the Sheriff wanted this time?

"Rich, I'm here again to ask you what you know about William Meredith? I want to know how his wallet and license showed up at you place?" he questioned.

"I told you before; I don't know how they got there," he said.

As he tapped his fingers nervously on the table, he continued to deny that he knew anything about Meredith and his belongings.

"I don't know how he got shot. I don't know anything about any of it!" Rich said. "If you want to know anything else, talk to my lawyer and don't be bothering me again."

"Well, Rich, how did you know that he was shot? I didn't mention it and it's not public knowledge," the Sheriff asked.

Rich was even more irritated at getting trapped by the Sheriff.

"I figured if he was a hunter and disappeared that he probably got shot. Hunters get shot sometimes. I'm not say anything else," he said.

Rich called for the guard and asked to go back to his cell. Shortly, Tom Aaron was brought in and the questioning started. Tom offered absolutely nothing in regard to William Meredith. He had no idea how the items got on their property.

"I told you the truth and that's all I'm saying," the agitated Tom said.

When the Sheriff was finished questioning him, he called the guard to take him back to his cell.

As he drove back to Mercyville, he was even more convinced that the Aarons knew something and were somehow involved in the case. It just seemed odd that Rich Aaron had brought up the fact that Meredith was shot when no one had mentioned it. With the body buried only a half-mile from the Aarons' cabin, it seemed possible they could have put it there. On the way back to the office he stopped to talk to Paul Devon.

The bell rang at the front desk and Paul went to see who had come in. He was surprised to see the Sheriff.

"Good after Dr. Devon. I just stopped by to let you know that I was over at the prison and questioned the Aarons'. Of course they denied any involvement. Rich Aaron made a slip and brought up the fact that Meredith had been shot. That information wasn't released to the public and even Mrs. Meredith doesn't know that yet," he said.

"I'm glad that you brought that up. Mrs. Meredith was here earlier. She just left a few minutes ago. She said you had called her after the body was recovered and identified. She wondered if I had any idea how her husband died. I told her I didn't know but as soon as the Coroner completed his report she should have an answer. I didn't know what you had told her so I'm glad that I didn't say anything," Paul remarked.

As soon as the Coroner releases the body for burial, she'll know the cause of death. I feel sorry for the poor women with all she's been through. I hope things start looking up for her. I'm headed back to the office. I'll keep you informed if we get any breaks in the case. The whole thing is very strange and it all seems to keep coming back to the Aarons.

After the Sheriff left, Paul closed the clinic for the day. Martin had taken Patch and gone home a few minutes before the Sheriff arrived. Just thinking about the whole incident made Paul shudder. He hoped the murder would be solved soon so everyone could put it behind them.

Martin was preparing dinner as Patch curled up next to the wood stove and went to sleep.

His cell phone rang and it was the electrician. He had a cancellation and asked Martin if it would be convenient to install this electrical on Friday. Martin said he would be there and Friday would work just fine.

As he continued cooking, he thought about the day and about Mrs. Meredith. It must have been pretty awful for her to look at the place where her husband was found. He hoped she could get over the experience soon. He could sympathize with her because he knew how he felt when the skull rolled out of the barrel and than found out that it was his father. It gave him chills just thinking about it. He had been so busy lately that he hadn't thought about it too much. He thought about the Aarons and how much he hated them. Being in jail is what they deserved, thought Martin. His thought was broken as his kerosene lamp started to flicker and then went out. He got the can of kerosene out and filled the lamp. As he re-lit the lamp he thought electricity was going to be a lot more convenient than filling the lamp. With the electricity on the way, he was considering getting a small refrigerator. The springhouse was fine for his needs but it was pretty inconvenient trudging through the snow in the winter. The next time I go to Edwardton, I'm going to look for a small refrigerator. There wasn't much more he needed to make life a little more comfortable. He was grateful for everything he had...especially Patch.

Friday morning the electrician arrived early at Martin's cabin. The cabin was only sixteen by twenty-four feet so it won't take long to wire and then modernization would be on its way. While the electrician was working, Martin decided to go to Edwardton and look at a refrigerator. With Franz coming tomorrow he would probably be tied up helping him for awhile. He put Patch in the truck and he headed toward town. When he got there he pulled up in front to the All Brands Appliance Store. The store carried the usual items; dishwasher, washers, dryers, stoves and refrigerators. A salesman asked him what he was looking for and then started showing him a line of way too large refrigerators. Martin reiterated that he only needed a small one. The salesman thought for a moment and said he had one in the basement that might suit his needs. He followed the salesman downstairs where several appliances were stored.

" This is the smallest one I have. It's been here for over two years. One of our customers ordered it and never came by to pick it up. People usually don't want anything this small, so I'll be glad to get rid of it. I can give you a really good price on it and if you take it yourself, you won't have to pay any delivery charges," the salesman said.

Martin said he would take it. He paid the salesman and the two of them started loading it in the back of his truck. As they were lifting it, a sales tag fell of the side of it and it read: Hold for William Meredith. Martin couldn't believe his luck. He just couldn't get away from the ghost of William Meredith. His mind slipped into overtime and he began to wonder if Meredith was trying to communicate something to him. The whole Meredith tragedy was now turning into a never-ending nightmare. As he drove back home from Edwardton, the continuing saga just kept playing out over and over in his mind. He thought for a man who minds his own business, he surely has the misfortune of getting involved in the strangest predicaments.

17

When Martin arrived at the Kohler homestead, he found Franz testing out the elaborate security system.

"Good morning, Martin, It seems like the house is ready to move in to! I am pleased with what the decorator has done and she seems to have thought of everything. How did things go while I was away?" Franz questioned.

"As you can see, everything arrived from the furniture company and the Decorator's warehouse. The cabin is also already to move in to. I put everything away over there while the decorator was working at the house," Martin said.

"Let's walk over and take a look at the cabin. I'm anxious to see how it all turned out."

When Franz opened the door, he was elated with the newly renovated cabin.

"I can't believe that this is the same cabin. My guests should be very comfortable here. By the way, I have a delivery truck coming from New York this afternoon. They said they would be here around noon. There are a lot of crates with paintings and sculptures in them. I would appreciate it if you could help me uncrate them when they arrive," he said.

"I don't have anything planned because I figured you would need some help when you got here," Martin replied.

"Are you still working for Dr. Devon?" asked Franz.

"I work for him part-time. When he needs me, he just calls me on my cell phone. We had a pretty bad thing happen at the clinic last week. We were building a barn behind the clinic and we were almost finished with it when Patch dug up a human skull," Martin said.

Franz's eyebrows went up with a look of shock as Martin proceeded telling him about the excavation of William Meredith. When he mentioned the name Meredith, Franz seemed even more concerned.

"Wasn't that the name on the license and in the wallet you found?" Franz questioned.

"Yes, it was the same person. The Coroner checked his dental records and it was Meredith for sure," Martin said.

"Does anyone know how he died or why he was buried on the Devons' property? The whole matter is very unsettling" Franz said.

"The Coroner said that he was shot in the head and the Sheriff thinks the Aarons are some how involved. They can't explain how the license and wallet got on their property. He believes they know a lot more than they are saying," Martin replied

"This is such a beautiful property here. I don't like having it associated with some of the things that are happening around here," he said. "When I bought the property, I knew about the kidnappings but I wasn't prepared for the other things that have been unfolding. I thought the Aaron brothers were just history and the whole thing would be forgotten but every time I come back something new turns up. I hope they keep the Aarons in jail for the rest of their lives. All of this news is very disturbing."

"Maybe this isn't a good time to ask, Mr. Kohler, but I was wondering if you decided about getting a snowplow?" Martin asked.

"Martin," Franz said, "If you need a snowplow, it's fine with me. I don't want to be snowed in this winter when I am up here. I'll give you a signed check and you can get what you think will work best for you. I almost forgot I made out a list of food and other grocery store items and I was wondering if you would go to Edwardton and get them?"

He reached in his wallet and handed Martin eight hundred dollars. "This should cover your wages for the last four weeks," he said. Then he signed a check for the grocery store and one for the snowplow.

"Just fill in the amount and bring the receipts back. Whenever you are here and spend any money of your own related to the property, keep the receipt and I'll reimburse you," Franz told him.

As Martin headed up the road toward Edwardton, he wondered how it must feel to have an endless supply of money. To him, it seemed like Franz would never run out of it. With eight hundred dollars in his pocket and two signed blank checks, Martin felt he had become the part-time handler of the never-ending Kohler money tree.

When he drove in to the Save Big Super Market parking lot he wondered if they had enough carts to hold the list Franz had given him. He also gave him free rein to get whatever else he felt they needed.

Two hours later, Martin had filled up six over flowing carts and a seventh half-full. With what he had just purchased, there was no doubt in his mind that the Save Big Market had surpassed their sales quota for the day. His only concern was whether he had enough room in the truck for everything. He had never seen that many groceries and paper products at one time in his life. Instead of folding the receipt, he had to roll it up and the cashier gave him a rubber band to hold the whole wad together! At the end of town, Martin stopped at the farmer's supply store. There he looked over the snowplows and decided on the one he felt would work best for him. He filled in the signed check and told the salesman that he would pick it up next week.

Driving back to Franz's, Martin thought that filling our signed checks was something he could very easily get used to!

The delivery truck from New York City was backed up to the house of extravaganza. Three men were carrying in various size crates. Martin decided to stock the cabin with the groceries until the delivery truck was finished. Fortunately, Martin bought two of everything; one for the house and one for the cabin. He marked the bags as the clerk packed each one so he could know what went where. Again, his organizational skills came into play. As he stacked the cupboards and refrigerator, he thought you could be snowed in here all winter and still have food left by spring. The truck from New York left just as he was finishing putting the groceries away.

He went over to the house and started unloading the remaining items from the truck. This was the first time he had been in the house since the carpenters had left. He was amazed at the size and openness of the rooms. In the living room, Franz was struggling to open one of the dozens of crates so Martin went out to his truck and brought in his toolbox. As Franz continued to open the crates, Martin stocked the kitchen, pantry and refrigerator. When he was finished with that, he started helping Franz unpack the heavy containers. As each one was opened, the living room started to look more and more like a museum. There were all sizes of bronze sculptures depicting horses, deer, dogs and figures in very reclining poses. Franz stacked dozens of gold-framed pictures against the wall until he decided where he wanted to hang them. Martin had never seen so much art. The closest to art he had seen lately were the framed pictures stacked in the barn collecting dust.

"After I get settled in here, I would like to invite the Devons over for cocktails. When I met Dr. Devon at the auction sale, he mentioned that his parents were avid art collectors," Franz remarked.

"I think the Devons would like that. They're really nice people. They weren't doing too well after their son, Joseph, died," Martin offered.

"I didn't know they had a son that died," Franz said.

Martin proceeded telling Franz the story of Joseph's death, Paul's accident and the kidnappings.

"Driving through Mercyville, you would never know all of these tragedies had occurred. It's such a peaceful, quiet village. Everyone I've met here, so far, seemed to be very pleasant. Of course, being a new arrival to the area I wouldn't have known about all that has happened here," Franz said. "I hope they get to the bottom of the Meredith case so everyone can put it out of their minds. I stopped over at the country store to get coffee this morning and I met several of the men there having coffee. I believe one said his name was Matt Wallace and he said both he and his wife were artists. I thought I would invite them over when I invite the Devons."

"I know Mr. Wallace. He's what the ladies of Mercyville call 'one of the opinion makers'."

Franz had a curious look on his face. He had never heard that term before.

"All of those men have coffee every morning and talk about anything they can think of. They seem to know everything that goes on around here. Mr. Wallace asked me to have coffee one morning but I was in a hurry and had to get some things done for Dr. Devon. They're real nice men. They were all upset when the kidnappings happened. All of them went out and helped search for the missing women. That was a bad time in Mercyville," Martin explained.

As Martin continued to unpack the objects of art, he asked Franz where he should put a grouping of bronze lions? Franz directed him to the built- in bookcase in the hallway. When Martin placed the heavy bronzes on the shelves, he could have sworn the bookcase moved. He didn't know if the carpenter's didn't finish their job or if he broke something when he put the heavy bronzes on the shelves. Whatever it was, he wasn't going to mention it to Franz. He thought he'd just let Franz put the art stuff away wherever he wanted it. He didn't want to have to pay for a broken bookcase and he surely didn't want to lose his job with Mr. Franz. Maybe I'll just stick to unpacking the crates; that seems a lot safer. I don't want to break anything else.

It was four o'clock and Patch had come up on the deck of the house and start barking, so Martin went outside to settle him down.

"Martin," Franz called, "We might as well quit for today. You've done enough for one day and I'm getting pretty tired. Tomorrow I'll just take my time and hang some of these paintings. I probably could use some help on Monday if you have time."

"That's all right with me, Mr. Franz. I'll be here in the morning," Franz said.

Martin was really tired and glad to be on his way home. As he was lying in bed, he kept thinking about the moving bookcase. He wondered if he imagined it or did it really move. He thought that maybe he should have said something to Mr. Kohler and than on the other hand, He thought if the bookcase is really broken, Franz would eventually find out for himself. He was just too tired to think any more.

Patch was asleep next to the stove and sleep is what He needed.

Part of the following week, Franz and Martin hung the dozens and dozens of paintings. Franz certainly knew what he was doing when he had the house designed with the massive amount of wall space. Paintings of every size filled a large portion of the walls. Across the heavy wood mantle on the fireplace, he arranged a series of bronze animals. On each end he placed deer and bear statues which were synonymous with the animals in the surrounding mountains. In the middle of the mantle, there was a bronze of a mountain lion and her cubs. On individual stands throughout the main floor of the house, were both marble and bronze statues of women with children, men in old fashion western attire, cowboys and Indians on horseback, a pack of howling wolves and busts of several women and mountain men.

Martin thought the off white walls had come alive with the brilliant colors of the Impressionist's paintings. He didn't know anything about art but he knew what he liked when he saw it.

When they had finished hanging the paintings in the living and dining areas, they started on the five bedrooms. Franz had specific paintings that he wanted in each room. It was obvious to Martin that the decor of each room had been planned to accentuate the paintings as their main focus.

Martin was fascinated by all of the art. The only thing he had ever done that was close to what he called art were the wood carvings of animals. After seeing the wild life bronzes, he thought he would like to get back to carving.

As they hung the last few paintings, he remembered the old paintings in the barn.

"Mr. Kohler, would you like me to bring the paintings in from the barn? I almost forgot about them being there," Martin said.

"We're finished here for today. Why don't we walk over to the barn and take a look at what's there," Franz suggested.

They separated the stack of paintings in the barn and stood them along the wall. Franz stepped back and carefully studied each picture. Most were old prints and three were slightly tattered old oils, which were in desperate need of cleaning.

"Martin, I don't think I want any of these. If you want them, please take them with you. You're going to have to clean those frames and the glass. I think if you use a slightly damp cloth on those oils, they may clean up well but don't use any harsh cleaning agents on them," he instructed.

"Thank you, Mr. Kohler. I'll take good care of them," Martin said.

Martin was slowly being drawn into the world of creativity. The domain behind the perimeters of his once sign covered fence no longer existed. In a little over two years, the gruff, unkempt loner had been replaced by a sensitive and caring individual.

"Now that we're finished with everything in the house, I'm going to call the Devons and the Wallace's and invite them over Saturday evening. Thank you, Martin for all of your help. I couldn't have gotten everything done without you," Franz said.

"If that's all you need me for, Mr. Franz, I think I'll head home," Martin said.

Martin backed his truck up to the barn and carefully loaded the old paintings. Once he applied his secret rub and scrub method, the paintings should look as good as new.

On the door of his cabin he found a note from the Power Company saying they had connected his electricity. When he walked inside, the first thing he did was to plug in his new, small, white refrigerator. Tomorrow he thought he would buy a few small lamps. The cabin would be perfect when he hung the pictures of his newly acquired art collection.

Life had been good to him he thought, as he opened a cola, sat at his kitchen table and listened to the quiet hum of his new white refrigerator.

Franz Kohler walked into Dr. Devon's clinic and introduced himself to the pregnant lady behind the desk.

"I'm Suzanne Devon, Paul's wife. We understand you are settling in to your new home. It certainly is nice to finally have a neighbor over there," she said.

"I came to invite you and Dr. Devon over Saturday night for cocktails. I want to invite Paul's parents and Matt Wallace and his wife. With the help of Martin Benson, I think I am finally settled in," Franz said.

Just then Paul came to the front desk and greeted Franz. He repeated his invitation to Paul and it was graciously accepted.

"We'll be there Saturday night. We are anxious to see your art collection. Martin said it is beautiful," Paul remarked.

"If I say so myself, it is a very fine collection. I was fortunate to have acquired some of the pieces I have. It's taken years of searching and collecting but it has been worth every minute of it.

Paul offered to show Franz through the clinic and barn.

"I understand from Martin, you had a very unfortunate incident here several weeks ago?" Franz said.

"Yes, it was a terrible shock to everyone. At least the disappearance of William Meredith has been solved and will bring some closure for Mrs. Meredith. There are still a lot of unanswered questions but I'm sure the Sheriff will eventually find out what happened and who is responsible for his death," Paul said.

"Thank you for showing me around, Dr. Devon. The clinic is very impressive and it seems you have thought of everything to make it a quality treatment center," he said.

"Please, Franz, call me Paul. Dr. Devon is rather formal for neighbors," Paul said.

As Franz left, Paul thought it was good to have a new neighbor and be rid of the Aarons. He still thought about what they had done to him and the two women from Mercyville. He shuddered every time he thought of how close he came to dying and how they had desecrated Joseph's sanctuary.

Martin had brought the old paintings in to the cabin and one by one started cleaning them. He particularly liked one small oil of a boy and a dog. He looked around the cabin and thought the best place for the painting would be above the four drawer cherry bureau. He stepped back and looked at the grouping. It was a perfect arrangement with the picture of his parents on the bureau and the painting hanging above it.

As he completed the transformation of each of the dusty paintings, he hung them around his cabin and when he was finished, he thought his cabin looked like a miniature version of Franz's art covered living room.

18

It was Saturday evening and Franz's first chance to entertain in his new home.

As the guests arrived they were ushered into the lavish living room with the art-covered wall. Even Charles Devon, an avid art collector himself, was impressed with Franz's superb collection.

"How long have you been an entrepreneur of fine art?" Charles asked.

"I started about thirty years ago buying for several well to do clients. After a few sales, my client list began to grow. Today I have approximately fifty clients I both buy and sell for. They express their interest in a particular artist or style of painting and then it is my job to find what they want. I have been on almost every continent procuring art. I started putting my personal collection together about the same time I began purchasing for my clients. I have lost count of the number of museums, brokers and auction houses I have dealt with over the years. It is a very interesting business," Franz said.

"We may be interested in having you purchase some pieces for us. I don't want Paul and Suzanne to know about it because we would like to give them a few paintings and sculptures as gifts for their new home. Paul is particularly fond of art depicting animals." said Rebecca Devon.

"I would be glad to purchase for you. There are several well-known auction houses planning major art sales over the winter. I will keep you informed as soon as I know what will be available." the knowledgeable Franz replied.

As Paul and Franz walked over to the fireplace the young doctor remarked."

"I love the animal bronzes on the mantle. Their compositions and the attention to detail are some of the finest I have ever seen."

Matt and Alison were overwhelmed by the size of Franz's collection. They had both been to many of the major art museums and galleries and were familiar with quality art.

"This is a superb collection, Franz. I love your choice of Impressionist paintings and the sculptures are exquisite. I would love my art students to have the opportunity to see your collection" Alison Wallace said.

"I'm sure we can arrange a time for them to come. Part of collecting is sharing it with others and helping them appreciate the beauty of art," he said.

The evening continued as Franz showed his guests through the house including the beautiful art centered bedrooms.

As the evening came to a close, it was obvious that Franz Kohler, dealer of fine art, had been well received by the residents of Mercyville.

Paul had decided to hire Mrs. Betty Meredith. Sitting all day had become uncomfortable for his pregnant wife. and he wanted her to get plenty of rest before the baby arrived. The next morning he called Betty Meredith and asked her to come to work for him. She accepted the offer and she would start as soon as he wanted her to.

A week later, Betty Meredith had become the latest member of the Devon Clinic.

Betty, like Martin, was a natural around animals. She assisted Paul and also took care of all the office matters. Paul wondered if having her husband's remains being found in the barn would be too upsetting for her but she seemed to have overcome the whole tragic situation. Her life was finally moving forward. Every time he went out to the barn, the excavation of Bill Meredith came back into his mind. Tomorrow Paul had a full schedule and he was happy that Betty was there to assist him. He called Martin and asked him to come in for the afternoon. Several large animals were coming in after lunch and Martin could handle the barn patients allowing him to concentrate on the office patients. Paul left the mornings open for surgery and any medical emergencies that might arise. Betty's ten-year experience with the Edwardton Animal Clinic was obvious as she assisted Paul during surgery. He thought he was fortunate to have found Betty or was it that Betty had found him?

It was one o'clock and Martin had not come to the clinic. He had told Paul that he would be there at twelve-thirty. It wasn't like him to be late so he tried to reach him on his cell phone but there was no answer. This concerned Paul but he would give Martin a little longer. The office was busy with patients, but fortunately Betty could handle most of the small animal appointments by herself. Without Martin, Paul would have to take care of the large animals in by himself.

By three o'clock, Paul was becoming very concerned about Martin not showing up. Just as he was getting ready to go and look for him, he heard Patch barking at the back door. He brought him inside and put him in a kennel. His first thought was that Martin might be over at Franz's. It was only a half-mile away and possibly Patch had run off and Martin was looking for him. He told Betty he was going over to the Kohler place and see if Martin was there. As he drove in the drive, there was no sign of his truck. When Franz answered the door, Paul asked if he had seen Martin?"

"No, I haven't seen him today. I wasn't expecting him today. We had finished with all of the unpacking and organizing of the house and cabin last week. I told him he didn't have to come over for a few days but if I decided I needed him, I would give him a call," he said.

"Was Patch over here this morning?" Paul questioned

"No, I didn't see him either and I've been here all day," Franz replied.

"Thanks a lot, Franz. I think I will run over to his cabin and see if he's there. It's really strange because he never goes anywhere without Patch and he showed up at the back door of the clinic," Paul said.

As Paul drove over to Martin's cabin, he had a very uneasy feeling about Martin not showing up. He parked his truck outside of the gate and walked up the private drive. He knocked several times and no one answered so he tried the door. It was unlocked, so he went inside and looked around. He couldn't help but think how neat and organized the cabin was. He looked at the paintings on the wall and for the first time he realized that Martin had an interest in art.

Paul closed the door of the cabin and decided to stop by the country store to see if anyone there had seen him. When he went inside, only two opinion makers were there. He asked if anyone had seen Martin but the answer was negative.

At this point, he had no idea where to look for him, so he went back to the clinic hoping Betty might have received a call from Martin. To Paul's dismay, she hadn't heard from him. He went back to the kennel and got Patch some food and water. I guess you'll be staying with me, boy, until we find your Master. I wish you could talk because I need some answers. Paul thought.

It was five o'clock when Paul closed the office and headed for home. When he got there, he explained the situation with Martin and wondered if he should call the Sheriff? He called his parents and asked their opinion. His father suggested that he should call the authorities and at least they could be on the lookout for Martin and his truck. The Sheriff felt that it was a little early to file a missing person's report but he would have his officers be on the lookout for Martin and the truck.

After twenty-four hours, Paul filed a missing person's report. He was very concerned about Martin's disappearance and he knew that he would have never left Patch alone for this long. He had a feeling that something terrible had happened to Martin but he hoped he was wrong.

Word spread quickly around Mercyville of the strange disappearance of Martin Benson. The conclave of opinion makers decided on their own to divide up and each search in a different direction. Franz Kohler had come in to the store in the morning for coffee and when he heard about the search he volunteered to go along with Matt Wallace. They all agreed that it was very unusual for Patch to show up but not Martin because he never went any place without his dog. They suggested that maybe Martin had been hunting and had some sort of accident. Since it was deer season, the country store put up a large sign with a description of Martin and his truck. They asked that the hunters be on the lookout for either one and report anything they found to the Sheriff. After a long period of calm, Mercyville was about to go back on the map of strange happenings.

Paul Devon asked his father and Ben Jenkins, the caretaker, if they would search the property at West Knob. Charles Devon had given Martin permission to hunt there and maybe he was somewhere on the estate. Possibly, Patch was with him, they had become separated and that was the reason why the dog showed up alone at the clinic.

Charles said he and Ben would go out right away and search the whole estate. With Ben's dog, Beau, if Martin was there, he would find him. Suzanne and Rebecca were very worried about Martin's safety. The whole situation brought back all of the memories of the kidnappings over two years ago and they hoped a similar fate had not fallen upon Martin.

The Sheriff had several of his officers go door to door around Mercyville letting people know about Martin and asking them to keep an eye out for him or his truck. He now had the entire force on the lookout for him throughout the county.

Even Miss Doris, the owner of the white poodle who had borne Patch's pups, stopped by Dr. Devon's office to ask if there was anything she could do the help? The good doctor thanked her and assured her if she could help in any way, they would contact her.

The wives of the opinion makers made platters sandwiched and took them to the country store for all of those involved in the search. The store provided beverages and said they would stay open as long as the searchers needed to be there. One of their own was in need of help and the village was going to be there for him.

After several hours, Matt and Franz were the first to return to the store. They had driven all the way down along the creek road, through the public lands and back. They didn't see any trace of Martin or his vehicle. The rest of the men of the conclave, returned throughout the afternoon with the same results as Matt and Franz.

Franz suggested to the Sheriff that maybe he should call the Save Big Super Market and the farmers supply store in Edwardton. He knew that Martin was going to pick up a snowplow there sometime during the week. The Sheriff acted on the suggestion and called the Edwardton police station. He asked them to check the two stores and see if he had been there. The day was coming to a close with no hints as to the whereabouts of Martin.

Back at the clinic, Paul noticed that Patch had become very somber and didn't eat. Something was definitely wrong and he had the suspicion that Patch was the only one who had the answer.

It had been over twenty-four hours and there had been no word from Martin Benson. All searches had been unsuccessful and the authorities were becoming concerned about his well being.

That night at Paul's home at White Deer Point, he went over and over searching his mind for any possible reason for Martin's disappearance. For as long as he had known him, he never knew him to shirk his obligations. He was always as good as his word.

"Suzanne, I am at a loss about Martin's disappearance. The only connection I have to him is Patch. I'm sure that dog knows where Martin is or what happened to him. It may be crazy but I'm going to take Patch out and search for Martin. I'll just start at the back door of the clinic and let Patch take the lead. At least I'll feel like I am doing something. Don't wait up for me as I'll probably be late," Paul told her.

Paul drove down to the clinic, got a lead line, put it on Patch and headed out of the back door. He noticed that the dog still had not touched his food and knew he was pining for his master. Outside, Patch was sniffing the ground then headed toward the woods behind the barn. Paul let him have the lead and held him on a loose line. It was all up to the dog now and Paul had faith that he would come up with something.

The moon was full, giving the pair a better view while going through the thick hemlock woods. Patch pulled tight on the lead line a kept his nose to the ground. He thought the dog was retracing his own tracks and if that was the case, there was still a chance of locating Martin.

After an hour of stopping, searching and circling, Paul started to wonder if this was just a midnight walk for Patch or if the dog knew something he didn't know. All of sudden, Patch gave a hard tug on the line and headed out of the woods to a clearing that opened up to Franz Kohler's property. The dog kept his nose to the ground and headed in the direction of Kohler's barn. At this point, Paul had to hold tight to the line as Patch pulled him forward toward the barn. When he reached the barn, the dog began to scratch on the door. Paul quietly opened the door and went inside. He shined his flashlight toward the far end of the barn and was shocked when he saw Martin's truck. It was partially covered with a large tarp. Patch pulled hard again on the lead line as he sniffed around all sides of the truck. Paul looked inside of the vehicle but there was no sign of Martin.

He was stunned by the discovery and his mind was racing wildly. Why would Martin's truck be here? Franz was helping to search during the day and surely he must of known that the truck was here. His stomach turned over and over as endless disastrous possibilities crossed his mind. Should he go back and call the Sheriff? As he stepped out into the quiet moonlit night, he pulled Patch's lead so that he was close by his side.

Out of the dark, a familiar voice told him not to turn around.

"Open the door and put the dog in the barn," commanded the voice. Paul felt the barrel of a gun in his back and did as he was told. It was the voice of his neighbor, Franz Kohler.

"I'm sorry, Dr. Devon, that you had to get involved in all of this. It wasn't my intention at all. If Martin hadn't been given that envelope which the carpenters found in the cabin, none of this would be happening. If only he wouldn't have looked inside, everything would have been all right. Now, I'm forced to do something I don't want to do," he said as he pushed the gun into Paul's back, he ordered him to walk forward.

"I have no idea what you are talking about! Where is Martin?" Paul demanded.

"Keep walking. You'll find out everything soon enough. I'm really sorry you had to pursue this search for Martin. You should have left well enough alone and you would have never gotten involved. Now, I have no choice as to what I have to do to you," Franz said.

Franz pushed the gun harder into Paul's back as they walked up the steps of the house of extravaganza. He opened the door, pushed Paul inside and forced him down the long hall. Halfway down the hall, he stopped and pushed a panel on the bookcase with the bronze statues. As the bookcase opened up, he shoved Paul in to the darkened room and closed the panel.

A voice came out the dark, it said, "Dr. Devon is that you?"

Paul still had his flashlight in his pocket and shined it in the direction of the voice.

"Martin? Are you all right? What happened? What's going on ? Everyone in Mercyville has been looking for you. Patch came to the clinic and when he was alone, I knew that something was wrong. How did you get here? Franz caught Patch and I coming out of the barn. I had him on a lead line and just let him go ahead. He headed through the woods and to the barn. I found your truck inside. When I stepped outside, Franz put a gun in my back and brought me here," Paul said.

"It's awful, Dr. Devon. I should never have come here when I did. I should have just come to the clinic," Martin said.

"Well, what happened? Why did he put you in here? I have no idea what is going on," Paul said.

"The carpenter found an envelope in the cabin when they tore out the old cabinets. They left it on the counter and the electrician gave it to me to give to Franz. I forgot I had and when I remembered, I thought I would stop and give it to Mr. Franz on my way to the clinic. As I got it out of my glove compartment in the truck, something fell out on the floor. I picked it up and it was an identification bracelet with William Meredith's name on it. Then I looked in the envelope. I wouldn't have looked in if the bracelet hadn't fallen out. It was any of my business," Martin told Paul.

"What else was in the envelope?" he asked.

"There was a copy of a check in it. It had been made out over two years ago to Tom Aaron for ten thousand dollars and it said 'for

Meredith' on it. Mr. Franz said I should never have looked in the envelope. When I asked him about the bracelet and the check, he pulled a gun out and put me in here. He said he had worked too hard to have his career ruined now and I didn't know what he meant," Martin explained.

"Why would he have made out a check for ten thousand dollars over two years ago to the Tom Aaron? I wasn't even aware that he knew them," Paul said.

"He said that a friend from New York asked him to go hunting with him. He saw an ad in the newspaper for the Aarons being hunting guides. He called them and that's how they got to Mercyville and the Aarons' cabin. It was his first time hunting and he thought he saw a deer and shot. He found out that he had shot William Meredith and said it was an accident. He said he panicked and he didn't want to loose his business and he didn't want any trouble with the police. He offered the Aarons ten thousand dollars to bury Meredith's body. When he heard the Aarons were in jail and their property was for sale, he bought it. He knew they would never say anything because they were in enough trouble," Martin explained.

"What about his friend who was with him? He certainly knows what happened to Meredith," Paul inquired.

"He said his friend had a heart attack two days after they got back to New York and died. He was the only one besides the Aarons that knew what had happened. He said it was too bad that I had to find the envelope. I think he is going to kill us. If only I wouldn't have looked in that envelope none of this would have happened. I'm sorry, Dr. Devon, you got involved. It's my entire fault," Martin said apologetically.

"No, it isn't your fault. It's Franz's fault. All of it. I can't believe how such a seemingly nice man could end up like this. Our biggest problem now is getting out of here alive. Are there any windows in this room?" Paul asked.

"Only way up at the top of the room and they are small. They let in a little light but not much. I remember when I was putting away Mr. Kohler's bronzes and put them on the shelf. I thought the bookcase moved and now I know it really did move and there was this room behind it. I never thought that Mr. Franz could do something like this," Martin said.

"Martin, let's just concentrate on getting out of here. Our lives don't mean anything to him. If he could kill Meredith and have him buried, he's not going to spare us. He's a man that won't stop at anything," Paul said.

Paul shined the flashlight around the room and saw stacks of paintings leaning against the walls. At the far corner of the darkened room there were two large packing crates. Then he shined the light up toward the windows.

"Do you think we could get out of those windows?" Paul asked.

"They look awfully small but you might be able to squeeze through one of them if you could get up to them," Martin replied.

"If we stacked those crates on top of each other and I stood on your shoulders, I think I can squeeze through," Paul said. "We don't have much choice, Martin, so we have to give it a try."

Quietly, the two men moved the large packing crates under the window and stacked them on each other. Martin stood on the crates and Paul pulled himself up on his shoulders. He could reach the window and felt around for the latch. Once he opened the window, he pushed himself through the tight space and was dangling about ten feet off of the ground. He had no choice now but to let go. He hit the ground hard but when he realized he was still in one piece, he quietly headed across the lawn, past the barn and out through the hemlock forest. When he reached the clinic, he called the Sheriff and told them everything that had happened. He informed them that Martin was still inside and they would have to approach quietly as not to arouse any suspicion. Martin's life depended on it.

When the officers arrived at the clinic, Paul explained to them where Martin was being held. They drove the half-mile to Kohler's place without lights and parked on the main road. Then they divided up and moved through the woods to the house.

The Sheriff went up to the front door and rang the bell. A sleepy Franz Kohler answered the ring. So to be sure Kohler wasn't armed he pretended he was just informing him of Martin's disappearance and would appreciate a call if he heard or saw anything pertaining to the missing man.

"Thank you, Sheriff. I was out today with Matt Wallace searching for Martin. I certainly hope they find him soon. As you know, he is my caretaker and an excellent worker," Franz volunteered.

The Sheriff could see both of Kohler's hands and knew he wasn't armed. In a fraction of a second, the unsuspecting Kohler was hit by the Sheriff and pushed to the floor.

"What are you doing?" Franz protested.

"I think you know why we are here," the Sheriff replied.

Another officer helped cuff Franz while Paul and two officers headed down the hallway to the bookcase. Paul called to Martin and immediately there was a response.

"I'm not sure how this bookcase opens," Paul said.

After several tries, he hit the right panel and the case slid to the side and the shaken Martin emerged unscathed.

"I was afraid you might not come back. I thought that maybe you got hurt when you jumped out of the window. Do you have Patch?" he asked

"He's in the barn, Go over and get him and your truck. When you come back, I think the Sheriff will want to talk to both of us."

Martin pulled his truck over near the house and when he got out, Patch didn't let him out of his sight. He followed him inside and sat next to him with his head on his lap as the Sheriff made out his report.

"You can thank Patch for finding you. I would never have thought to look at Franz's, especially since he was out looking for you all afternoon. It is hard to understand how someone you are so sure is a decent human being could do what Franz did. It makes you wonder how far some people will go to get what they want," Paul remarked.

"I never thought Mr. Franz could do anything like this. He was always nice to me until I told him about the envelope and I asked him about the bracelet. If that bracelet hadn't fallen out, I would have never looked in the envelope," Martin said.

"Martin," said the Sheriff. "If it weren't for you, we may have never found out who killed William Meredith. At least we can tell his wife what happened and give her the bracelet and we can finally put this case to rest. The only thing I don't know is who put the license and wallet at the Aarons' cabin. They say they didn't do it and now I'm wondering if Kohler did it. We'll find out sooner or later."

"If that's all you need from Martin and I, I'm going home. It's been a long, long day. I'm sure Martin needs to get some rest too," he said.

"No, go on home. I'll be talking to both of you again soon," the Sheriff stated.

Patch and Martin got in the truck and headed home. Paul followed them as far as West Knob where he headed down the long driveway toward White Deer Point.

As Paul went in to the bedroom, Suzanne was awake.

"I was worried about you. You've been gone for hours. I was about to call your parents," she said.

"Suzanne, it's been a long night and I'm too tired to explain everything now. Martin is safe and I'll explain everything in the morning. What I need now is sleep," Paul said.

When Martin arrived home, he put wood in the stove, started a fire and crawled in to bed. In the dark of the night, he could hear Patch crunching his food and drinking his water. In a few minutes, he went over and lay down near the stove. At last the cabin was back to being a home again.

The next morning, the Devons were having a late breakfast. Ben Jenkins had been invited to join them. Everyone sat half stunned as Paul explained the whole episode of the night and early morning. Charles shuddered at how close his son had come again to dying.

"Franz seemed like such a nice man. He had everything he wanted," Rebecca Devon remarked.

"Maybe that is why he was afraid of losing everything. He had it all and he wasn't going to let anyone stand in his way of getting more. Martin is lucky Franz didn't shoot him right away. The whole thing is hard to believe. Never in a million years would I have ever conceived something like this happening. I hope Martin is going to be all right. This whole experience could send him right over the edge! I mean first becoming involved in the kidnappings, then that barrel/skull thing and finding out it was his father, then digging up William Meredith's body! This experience with Kohler abducting him combined with everything else, might be just too much for him to handle. I'm afraid Martin may go right off the deep end!" Charles Devon said.

"I think Martin is going to be all right. The thing that will keep him going is Patch. If he didn't have that dog, it might be different. I'm just afraid that it is going to take him a long time to start trusting people again. I'm going to give him a call later and ask him to meet me for lunch at the recreation ground. I don't want to see him sitting alone out at his cabin and start thinking too much about everything that has happened. I'm going down to the clinic and tell Betty Meredith what happened. She was concerned about Martin too."

I hope this is the end of the Meredith case," Paul said.

When he went to the clinic, he asked Betty to come in to his office.

"Betty, have a seat. I have some more news about your late husband," he said.

He proceeded to tell her that Martin was safe and everything that happened the night before. He wasn't sure how she would take this latest development.

"Dr. Devon, I'm almost shockproof now. Bill has been dead for so long and finding the body put closure to the past two years. After several weeks and he hadn't come home, I resigned myself to the fact that he was never coming back. I am glad to know who killed him. If only Mr. Kohler would have turned himself in when it happened, it would have been a whole lot easier to understand. Unfortunately, hunting accidents happen but I can't forgive him for what he did. The Aarons are just as much to blame as Mr. Kohler is," Betty said.

"I almost forgot," Paul said. "Martin found an identification bracelet with your husband's name on it. The Sheriff is going to return it to you.

"I'm going to call Martin and ask him to meet me for lunch. I'd like you to join us."

"I'd be glad to go along. I was wondering how Martin is holding up?

He's been through so much lately," she said.

"That's why I want to get him out of his cabin and start getting back with people as soon as possible. It's not good for him to be alone and start thinking about everything right now," Paul said.

As the trio entered the recreation ground restaurant, friends wished Martin well and expressed how glad they were to see him back and safe.

"You know, Dr. Devon, if it weren't for you, I might be dead by now. The whole time I was locked in that room the only thing that kept going through my mind was a picture of the white buck deer. I just couldn't think of anything else except the white deer. It was very strange," Martin remarked.

"Well, Martin, if it weren't for you, I might be dead too," Paul said. "If you weren't in that room, I could never have gotten up to that window. I have a feeling that the spirit of the white deer was watching over us. The whole incident is almost too hard to comprehend. I'm just glad it's all over. If you're up to it, I have a few things that need to be done back at the clinic. If you want to come back after lunch that will work out fine for me...only if you feel up to it though. Besides I have a paycheck to give you."

Martin went back to the clinic and worked all afternoon. Patch stayed near him and didn't let him out of his sight. They almost lost each other once and neither dog nor man was going to let it happen again!

19

A week after the abduction of Martin and Paul, the Sheriff stopped by the clinic. Betty Meredith was at the front desk when he came in.

"Mrs. Meredith, I stopped by to see Dr. Devon and to give you this." He reached in his pocket and handed her the identification bracelet that had belonged to her husband. "I am sorry I had to return it to you under such tragic circumstances, but I thought you would want it," the Sheriff said.

"Thank you Sheriff. I'm glad to get it back. It is a remembrance of Bill. I appreciate you dropping by," she said.

"Is the doctor in?" he asked.

"Yes, he's in his office. I'll tell him you are here," she said.

"Sheriff, he said to go back to his office. It's straight down the hall and to the right," she said.

"Have you and Martin recovered yet from the Kohler experience?" he asked

"Well, we're getting on with our lives. I was very concerned about Martin but so far he is doing fine. I have been trying to keep him busy here at the clinic," Paul remarked.

"I'm glad you are sitting down, Doctor, because I have some very interesting news for you about Franz Kohler," the Sheriff said.

Paul stared at the Sheriff with a puzzling look on his face as he started to speak and not knowing what to expect.

"Our friend, Franz Kohler, is not the person he presented himself to be. To start with, his name is not Franz Kohler. His name is Jeff Steven Stone. When we ran his fingerprints, Stone came up. He had spent six years in prison for art forgery. He has a rather long rap sheet, including swindling, art forgery, impersonating himself as museum art procurer and a long list of other offenses. He has been using the name Kohler for the last ten years. He had quite a long list of wealthy clients for whom he had been procuring art.

"The problem is that ninety percent of the art he has are fakes. He had two men who forged almost every painting he ever sold. One French client became suspicious when she found a near duplicate of her purchase in the window of a New York City shop. He has been living the high life for years. I'm very surprised he wasn't caught for his art dealings before now.

"This explains why he didn't want to get involved with the police when he shot William Meredith. Evidently, he put all of his money in this house, furnishings and property. He was preparing to increase his client list. The New York City police picked up the two men who were doing the forgeries for him and they aren't too happy with Kohler, I mean Stone. He owes them quite a bit of money.

"He's been talking to a lawyer and he has to sell the property to pay for his legal fees. He's going to have to have a lot of money and some pretty good lawyers to get him out of this. With a murder and two counts of kidnapping, I don't think he is going to be involved in any art dealings in the near future. The only thing close to art he'll be doing is painting cells. I really shudder at how close you and Martin came to getting shot. Kohler had nothing to lose by killing you two. He was almost at the end of his bank account and he wasn't about to let anything stand in his way of refilling it. What goes around finally came around for Stone. He got what he deserved and by getting that envelope, the whole operation fell apart," the Sheriff concluded.

"I'm so overwhelmed by all of this; I don't know what to say. Even my father, who is an avid collector, was fooled by Franz's collection," Paul admitted.

"There's no denying it was a very polished operation. They were good, very good, at least that's what the New York detectives are saying. It's a good thing he's in jail because he has taken a lot of people for a lot of money and I'm not talking about thousands, I'm talking about millions of dollars in the past ten years. He traveled all over the world on someone else's dime. I have to be on my way now but I thought you would want to know all of this. I think when you tell Martin about the former Franz Kohler, he should feel pretty good about his part in breaking up the whole operation. Give my regards to Martin," he said, as he left the office.

"Dr. Devon, is everything all right? You look a little pale," Betty asked.

"I'm fine, Betty. Just a little bit surprised at everything I just heard. We don't have any more patients today, so why don't we close the office. You can get home a little earlier today. I'll see you in the morning," Paul said.

When Paul arrived home, Suzanne was at his parent's house at West Knob. Charles, Rebecca and his pregnant wife were all in the living room when he walked in.

"You're home early today," Suzanne said.

"Well, my dear family, I'm glad you are all here. I have something to tell you and I don't want to have to repeat this story more than once."

With that said, Paul had their undivided attention.

As he repeated what the Sheriff had told him, a wave of disbelief spread over the Devons. When he finished with the most recent chapter involving Martin and himself, he jokingly broke the silence and asked if anyone had any questions?

The whole Devon clan sat in the living room stunned beyond words.

Rebecca was the first to speak, she said, "You won't believe this, but I was ready to purchase a few paintings and sculptures through him for you and Suzanne for a house-warming gift. I hate to say this, but our Mr. Kohler really had me baffled. I was totally enveloped in this whole art-purchasing scheme. I never suspected a thing. I'm certainly glad I didn't give him any money."

"I'm sorry you and Martin became involved in the whole mess but I am thankful it turned out the way it did. A lot of people owe a lot to Martin. If it weren't for him getting that envelope, Franz Kohler, or whatever his name is, would still be conning a lot of people out of millions of dollars. I was totally impressed by that art collection of his. I am certainly going to have to be more careful from now on when I am considering any art purchases. The thought of paying thousands of dollars for a lot of worthless paintings and sculptures has put the fear of God in to my art procurement. I'm glad you and Martin got out of this whole thing alive! Do you have any idea who Kohler's lawyer is?"

" No, Dad, I have no idea. The Sheriff didn't mention a name but I suppose if you give him a call he can tell you that. If he doesn't know, I'm sure he can find out for you," Paul suggested.

The people of the village were elated that Martin Benson and Paul Devon had come through the Franz Kohler experience unscathed. They thought that was the end of another Mercyville disaster, but when the history of Kohler and his art operation were exposed, the phones and the emails were tearing up the wires all over the county.

The conclave of opinion makers had enough ammunition to keep the oversized table warm and the coffee machine going for weeks. When Martin came in to the country store for his weekly supply of cola, he was treated as though he had won the hundred-million-dollar lottery! The men of the conclave treated him to so many cups of coffee that when he finally left the store; he was shaking like a hula dancer in a hurricane. They wanted every detail of the saga straight from the horse's mouth. After explaining so many unfortunate incidents of the past two years, Martin was slowly gaining the finesse and confidence of a professional storyteller. The opinion makers wanted to hear every detail and sat on the edge of their seats waiting for the grand finale!

Matt Wallace was probably the most shocked of the group as it was he and Franz who went together searching for Martin. He was the most hurt by the ploy of sincerity about finding Martin when all along he knew he was locked up at his house.

When Alison Wallace found out about the whole Kohler affair, she felt embarrassed at having been so naive and gullible to be taken in by all of the glitz and glamour.

The Wallace's and the Devons weren't the only ones taken in. At least they didn't have any money invested like dozens and dozens of other people. The only thing they lost was a temporary trust in human beings but they had gained a great lesson in character evaluation.

Martin walked in to the clinic and told Betty he needed to speak to Dr. Devon. Betty sent him back to his office.

"Come on in. I was just checking over a few of these reports. What can I do for you?" asked Paul

Well, I don't know what to do about that snowplow I got in Edwardton. Mr. Kohler paid for it and now I don't know what to do with it. It really isn't mine. So what do you think I should do?" Martin asked.

"I don't think that's a big problem. Franz isn't going to be using a snowplow in jail. You'll probably have to plow at the Kohler place until they figure out what's going to happen to the property. For now, Martin, I wouldn't worry about it. Just use it and enjoy it. With what you have been through, you deserve twenty snowplows. And by the way, Franz didn't pay for it. The people he conned out of their money paid for it. If the Sheriff thinks it should be returned, then we'll just take care of that when it happens. In the mean time, the way I see it, you've got yourself a new snowplow. The Sheriff or Franz's lawyers will probably ask you to take care of the house and cabin just to make sure that the heat is working, the pipes don't freeze and just making sure everything is kept in good shape over the winter. I think you'll have a lot to keep you busy this winter," Paul said.

Late fall turned into an early winter for Mercyville. Everyone knew it would happen when they spotted the brown caterpillars crawling on their houses and around the their doorframes.

Martin was extra busy cutting wood for those of the village who had wood stoves and fireplaces.

Dr. Devon's clinic was busy treating the animals in and around the mountains of Mercyville. He was glad that he was busy so the time went faster and he was that much closer to becoming a first time father. Suzanne was due to have their child around Christmas. At his home at White Deer Point, his wife was busy preparing for the holidays and the baby. Everyday he came home from the clinic, Suzanne had decorated another room with pinecones, branches, red ribbons, Christmas ornaments and mounds of holly and red candles on each of the fireplace mantels.

Charles and Rebecca Devon were planning a drop-in Christmas party for their family and friends and were looking forward to the hoiidays.

All through the Endless Mountains, signs of Christmas began to appear on the lawns, in the windows, on the front doors and draped around the trees. It seemed as though the discount mart had a rush on every kind of electric strand of lights in stock. No one held back on their outdoor decorations and even Martin, for the first time, had a wreath on the door of the cabin and electric candles in the windows. Dr. Devon had ordered pet sweaters to sell in the clinic and those were going fast. Of course Martin's companion, Patch, had to be one of the first to be included on the list of best-dressed dogs in Mercyville. Betty Meredith had put up Christmas decorations around the waiting room of the clinic and baked dozens of dog recipe cookies for the patients.

Martin was making use of the snowplow by keeping the clinic parking lot clear and occasionally he would go to Franz's place to plow the ever-drifting snow in the driveway.

Rebecca had invited Martin and Betty to their drop-in party along with friends from the village.

Things were relatively back to order in the village, but with the past disasters they had experienced, the locals were a little more on guard.

Dr. Devon and his wife invited Martin and Betty for a holiday lunch at the Edwardton Hotel. It had been newly renovated and sported a Victorian decor which blended in with the historic district of the town.

After the meal, gifts were exchanged along with holiday cheer. Martin, who rarely indulged in alcoholic beverages, gave in to a glass of white wine.

Martin handed Paul and his wife a large box neatly wrapped in Christmas paper. Paul opened the package and was taken back by what he saw. He lifted out a glass case with a white buck deer inside standing on a cherry wood pedestal.

"Where did you get this Martin?" the surprised doctor asked.

"I carved it for you and Mrs. Devon. I hope it's good enough," Martin said shyly.

"This absolutely beautiful. It's one of the finest carvings I have ever seen. I had no idea that you could carve. Thank you very much. Suzanne and I will cherish this forever," he said. "We have a gift for you and Betty."

Martin opened his first and found a beautiful red goose down jacket and fur mittens.

"We thought you would need this to go along with your snowplow," Paul laughed.

Betty handed Suzanne a colorfully wrapped box. Inside was an absolutely stunning handmade gingerbread house that had been sprayed to preserve it for many years. Then she handed Martin his gift.

"I hope you like it. I made it myself," she said.

It was a handsome red and black knit scarf and hat.

"It looks like I'm going to be well dressed for winter and snowplowing," Martin said with a smile.

"I have a gift for you too, Betty," Martin told her as he handed her a box wrapped in silver and gold Christmas paper. She opened the gift and was pleasantly surprised at a carved wood mare and colt. Like the Devons' gift, it to was on a cherry wood pedestal in a glass case. When she opened her gift from the Devons she found a lovely hand knit Scandinavian sweater with matching gloves.

"This is the happiest time I have had in over two years. I thank all of you for the beautiful gifts and for your friendship," she said.

It was Saturday evening when friends begin arriving at the Devons' Christmas party. Betty Meredith arrived in her new Scandinavian sweater followed a little while later by Martin who was donned in his red goose down jacket and accessories. When most of the partygoers were there, Charles Devon said he had an announcement to make.

"I don't usually make an announcement like this sort of thing at a party, but since so many of our friends from Mercyville are here, I thought I would make an exception. I have purchased the former Franz Kohler property. I bought it for my grandsons and for our soon-to-be grandchild," he said.

"Dad, how come you didn't tell me?" Paul asked.

"Sometimes we have to keep things secret and a surprise. I didn't even tell your mother. And Martin, if you'll come over here, I have something for you," Charles said.

Martin was embarrassed as he made his way over to Mr. Devon. Charles handed him a legal folder. These are the legal papers I had drawn up by my lawyer giving you the Kohler cabin to live in free for the rest of your life. I will pay all of the expenses but I would ask you to keep up the grounds as long as you are able. I also understand that you have a snowplow whose ownership is in question. (Martin felt a twinge of guilt over the snowplow issue.) That now belongs to you along with a new truck to attach it to and that is in the papers too. After all, you'll be taking care of my grandchildren's new property.

Martin was in a state of total surprise, he said, "I don't know what to say, Mr. Devon." "Martin, all you have to say is yes," he said.

"Well, yes. I would like that very much," Martin stammered.

"Oh, by the way, I saw that beautiful white deer you carved for Suzanne and Paul. If you want any of the art works in the house for your cabin, go over there and help yourself. Well, I think that's about all I have to say for this evening. Let's party!" Charles said.

A round of applause sounded throughout the Christmas spirit filled mansion. Outside Patch was laying on the porch next to Ben Jenkins dog, Beau. Both were dressed in their Christmas sweaters as a few snowflakes started to fall on two very lucky dogs.

After everyone left the party, Rebecca kicked off her shoes and joined Charles in front of the fireplace.

"Why didn't you tell me you were going to buy the Kohler place?" she asked.

"I didn't say anything until I was absolutely sure it was ours. I had to wait on Kohler's lawyers to draw up the final papers. I made an offer on the whole property, including all of the contents. Franz wasn't in any position to hem and haw too long. He needed lawyers and as you know lawyers want money…a lot of it. I really don't think Franz or whatever his name is, will be getting out of jail for many years. I felt that Martin deserved the cabin. Actually, a lot of people owe him a lot more than a cabin. Franz, whoever he is, was stopped just in time and the thanks go to Martin. Let's go to bed. It's been a long day and I'm not getting any younger!"

The week after the Devons' Christmas party, Martin started moving in to his new cabin at the former Kohler property. When he first saw the cabin, after it was renovated, he never imagined he would be living there. He didn't have much to move out of his cabin as he had decided to rent it out to hunters or tourists. He just took his clothes and old paintings that he had found in Kohler's barn.

With the truck loaded up with his belongings, he turned the key in the door, looked out over his property and closed the book on the past.

Patch was lying in front of the new fireplace as Martin turned the cabin in to a mini art gallery. He had picked out a number of paintings and sculptures from the house and gave them a new home over at the Benson's residence.

He had put his Christmas wreath on the front door and the electric candles in the windows. In the corner of the living room, he put a small pine tree. He had made a special trip to Edwardton and purchased ornaments for his first Christmas tree. On the fireplace mantel, he had placed the picture of his Mother and Father and on the very end of the mantel there was a red and green stocking with name Patch stitched in white letters.

As he sat on the new cranberry plaid sofa, in front of the fireplace, he thought of how lucky he was. He barely remembered the Martin that had lived behind the perimeters of his sign covered fence. He thought of all the people who had reached out to him and offered a caring hand of friendship. He wondered how he could ever repay them for their kindness. His thought was interrupted as Patch went over to the front door and let out a long, low growl. He looked out of the window and in the moonlight, he thought he saw a white buck deer walking across the snow in front of the cabin. The deer stopped, turned around and looked directly at the cabin then faded into the hemlock forest.

The next day at the clinic, Dr. Devon told Martin of a strange thing that had happened the night before.

"I was lying in bed and for a few seconds, I could almost swear, that in the room, I saw, in spirit form, the white deer. I got up and looked out of the window and down below in the moonlight, I thought I saw a white buck deer slowly walking out toward the cemetery then fade into the hemlocks. I still don't know if it was a dream or if it actually happened. It was the strangest experience I have ever had," Paul said.

"Dr. Devon, I think that the spirit of the white deer has come back to the mountains. This is his home and where he was born. I always thought that the Aarons killed the white deer and he brought his wrath down on them. Anyone, who kills the white deer, kills his own spirit and soul. I think his spirit has spread across Mercyville," Martin told Paul.

Martin never mentioned that he had seen the white buck at his new cabin because now he wasn't sure if he really saw it or imagined it.

When he went for his weekly supply of cola at the country store, Matt Wallace was telling the conclave of opinion makers that he thought he had seen the white deer the night before at his house. It was the strangest thing. He just looked at the house and then faded into the woods.

Martin was more sure than ever that the spirit of the white buck deer had come back and was spreading his blessing over the village of Mercyville.

20

It was Christmas Eve and almost everyone from Mercyville was going to Martin Benson's first party. He had never been given a party in his life nor had he ever hosted one. To show his appreciation to the people of the village he invited everyone to his first party to share in the celebration of his new life. He had asked Betty to help him with the party. From, Edwardton, they ordered trays of sandwiches, Hors D'oeuvres, French pastries, relish trays and salads. Betty made dozens and dozens of decorated Christmas cookies. Together she and Martin made small favors of red baskets filled with Christmas candy and on the handle of each basket there was a small statue of a white deer.

The new cabin was filled with the spirit of the holiday season. Charles and Rebecca Devon were among the partygoers but Martin was disappointed that Dr. Devon and his wife hadn't come to his premiere party. As the clock struck twelve, another Christmas had arrived. Ten minutes later, Martin's phone rang. It was Paul Devon and he asked to speak to either his Mother or Father. Charles took the call and then hung up. He said that he had an announcement to make. The room of guests became silent as Charles took the floor.

"Martin, I know you are disappointed that Suzanne and Paul aren't here. I wanted to explain why when we first arrived, but you know how I like surprises. With that call, I can now announce the birth of our first granddaughter and the Devon family's first Christmas baby, Christina Lynn Devon," he announced.

A round of applause and congratulations filled the cabin.

Martin turned to Betty and said, "I guess I can forgive Dr. Devon and his wife for not coming to the party. It seems as though they had a more important party of their own!"

As the guests left Martin's first party and fanned out across the village, they carried the handmade favors with the small statue of the white buck deer. The day after Christmas, when Dr. Devon went to his office, he found, sitting on his desk, three red baskets filled with candy and a small white deer on the handle.

Five days after Martin's Christmas party, the Sheriff stopped by the clinic. Martin and Paul were standing in the waiting room talking when the front door opened and the sound of sleigh bells, on the front door, filled the air.

"I just thought I would let you know that the former Franz Kohler admitted that he hid the wallet and the license at the Aarons. He said he slipped the wallet through the crack in the steps and later put the license out in the barn. He thought no one would ever find them. For once, the brothers were telling the truth. As I was driving over here, the strangest thing occurred. A doe, with a pure white yearling, crossed the road right in front of me and headed toward West Knob. In all of my years of driving around these mountains, that was the first time that I have ever seen a pure white deer," he said.

Martin and Paul just looked at each other.

"Well, Sheriff," said Dr. Devon, "Maybe today is just your lucky day."

21

The winter in Mercyville passed slowly. Most of the residents were pretty well snowbound for a good part of the winter. Travel was hazardous if you were caught in a sudden snow storm while going over the mountain to Edwardton. But, the people of Mercyville were used to the bad winters and took them in their stride. The telephone lines were filled with the news of the village. Emails hummed their way around the country letting all of their friends and relatives know "Yes, we have plenty of food, or of course we won't go outside in this weather and no, we don't want to move to Florida."

Martin Benson was enjoying his new art decorated home and when he wasn't plowing snow, he immersed himself in his wood carving. Word of his renewed talent had spread fast and people were anxious to purchase a Benson original. The Edwardton paper did an article on Martin and his animal carvings. People from as far away as New York, after reading the article, were calling to place orders. It seemed that he was definitely in demand and his creative orders were full for the next year. He seldom made anything for himself but he did make one special carving of Patch which he placed on the mantel, next to the picture of his parents.

Charles Devon liked Martin's work so much that he ordered an array of wild animals from him and had a special glass cabinet made to display them in his living room. At least with Martin's work, he knew he was getting an original, which couldn't have been said about Franz Kohler and his art.

Dr. Devon and Suzanne were joyous over the birth of their

daughter and of course Rebecca Devon could not buy enough for her first granddaughter. Rebecca lavished her grandchildren with every conceivable thing she could purchase on her trips to Philadelphia.

There seemed to be no end to the spending for the Devon grandchildren.

Ben Jenkins, the Devons' caretaker, decided to take a trip to a warmer climate for a few weeks. He ended up like most northerner's — you guessed it — Florida. When he returned to Mercyville he was sporting a tan which he picked up in the Sunshine State and decided that would be his last trip to Florida. Being born and raised in Mercyville, he was used to fewer people and driving on I-95 was more than he could stand. The whole time he was in Florida, he never did figure out where everyone was going in such a big hurry.

At the clinic Betty Meredith was busy and happy to be working with animals. The list of clients had grown and Dr. Devon needed Martin's help more than ever. It seemed that more and more new people were moving into Mercyville and everywhere you looked second homes were flooding the landscape along with their pets.

The recreation ground was planning on an influx of tourists for the summer and was making room for even more camping trailers. Their reputation for great pizza had spread for miles around and they had to order another oven.

The biggest change in Mercyville was at the country/store post office. Since the conclave of opinion makers had out grown their oversized round table, a huge new table, with twice the space, was being made. The men were still solving the problems of the country over their morning coffee and there never seemed to be an end to the conversations. The only interruptions were when one of the wives called the store and ask their husband to bring some grocery item home.

All and all it seemed that Mercyville was back to normal as it slid into spring. The newborn cubs and fawns started to wonder out from the security of their mothers and if you were lucky you might get a glance at the newest arrivals.

There was one change even bigger than the new round table at the country store. On a warm spring day, at the Devons' mansion at West Knob, Martin Benson and Betty Meredith became husband and wife.

As they drove off on their honeymoon, Martin had to slow down to let a doe and her new born white fawn cross the road.

Printed in the United States
28105LVS00001B/403-423

Traudl, à deux ans environ, avec sa mère Hildegard Humps.

Vacances d'été sur l'Ammersee, vers 1927. De gauche à droite : Traudl Humps, une camarade de jeu et Inge Humps ; à l'arrière-plan : Agathe Zottmann, la grand-mère.

Avec son amie Ulla Kares, 1940.

Collaboratrice de la chancellerie du Reich à Berlin, 1942.

Mariage avec Hans Junge, 19 juin 1943.

Les jeunes mariés, Traudl et Hans Junge, avec leurs témoins,
Otto Günsche (à gauche) et Erich Kempka (à droite).

Dans le « train spécial » du Führer : Traudl et Hans Junge avec Johanna Wolf (à droite) en train de regarder les photos du mariage.

Adolf Hitler avec son aide de camp, Hans Junge, au début des années 40.

© Walter Frentz.

Sur la terrasse du Berghof, en 1943. Assis, de gauche à droite : le lieutenant-colonel Gerhard Engel, Heinrich Hoffmann (derrière lui, Traudl Junge), Walther Hewel, Gerda Bormann (de dos) et le secrétaire d'Etat au tourisme Hermann Esser.

© Walter Frentz.

En conversation avec Sepp Dietrich, 1943.

Rituel du soir : le raccommodage de bas dans sa chambre du quartier général du Führer, la « Tanière du loup », 1943.

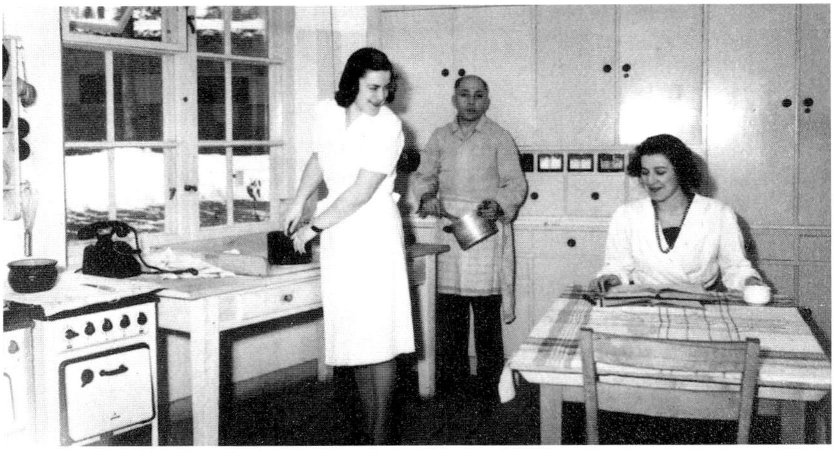

Dans la cuisine de la Tanière du loup, on préparait exclusivement de la nourriture diététique pour Adolf Hitler. De gauche à droite : Marlene von Exner, l'aide-cuisinier Wilhelm Kleyer et Traudl Junge, fin 1943.

Photo pour la nouvelle carte d'identité,
Berlin, novembre 1945.

Traudl Junge avec son fiancé Heinz Bald, 1955.

II.

In der "Wolfschanze"

Es dauerte verhältnismässig kurze Zeit, bis ich mich in dieser neuen, fremden Welt eingewöhnt hatte. Allerdings war die Natur, der Wald und die Landschaft eine grosse Kupplerin in meinen Beziehungen zur neuen Arbeitsstätte. Es gab keine Büroatmospühre, keine feste Arbeitszeit, ich machte weite Spaziergänge und genoss den Wald. Keine Sekunde hatte ich Sehnsucht nach der Grosstadt.

Hitler selbst behauptete zwar, man habe das billigste, sumpfigste, mückenreichste und klimatische ungünstigste Gebiet für ihn ausgesucht, aber ich fand es herrlich. Zumindest im Winter hatte die Ostpreussische Gegend einen unbeschreiblichen Reiz. Die verschneiten Birken, den klaren Himmel und die Weite der Ebenen mit ihren Seen werde ich nie vergessen. Im Sommer allerdings musste ich meinem Chef zu einem grossen Teil recht geben, denn Myriaden von Mücken hausten mit uns und ernährten sich von unserem Blut. Die Luft war dumpf und feucht und manchmal atembeklemmend. Bei solcher Witterung war es schwer, Hitler zu seinem täglichen Spaziergang zu bewegen. Er verkroch sich in seinem kühlen Bunker und nur seinem Hund Blondi zuliebe unternahm er nach dem Frühstück einen Rundgang in dem kleinen Gelände, das anschliessend an seinen Bunker für diesen Zweck reserviert war. Hier musste die Schäferhündin ihre Kunststücke zeigen und wurde von ihrem Herrn zu einem der gelehrigsten und gewandtesten Hunde ausgebildet. Hitler hatte das grösste Vergnügen, wenn Blondi ein paar Zentimeter höher springen konnte, wenn sie ein paar Minuten länger auf einer schmalen Stange balancieren konnte und behauptete, die Beschäftigung mit seinem Hund sei seine beste Entspannung. Es war auch erstaunlich, was Blondi leistete. Sie sprang durch Reifen, überwand eine 2 m hohe Holzwand spielend, kletterte eine Leiter hoch und machte oben auf der kleinen Plattform ihr schönstes Männchen. Es war wirklich eine Freude, zu beobachten, mit welchem Vergnügen Herr und Hund diese Übungen verfolgten. Am Rande des Geländes fanden sich manche Zuschauer ein, die das Spiel beobachteten und auch für mich war es wochenlang die einzige Gelegenheit, bei der ich mit dem "Führer" in Berührung kam. Wenn er mich sah, begrüsste er mich freundlich mit Händedruck und fragte mich, wie es mir ginge.

Original du manuscrit de Traudl Junge datant de 1947.